KILLIONAIRE

Published June 2026

by Indies United Publishing House, LLC

Edited by Jen Marshall

Cover Art by Craig Brown

FIRST EDITION

ISBN: 978-1-64456-923-8 [Hardcover]
ISBN: 978-1-64456-924-5 [Paperback]
ISBN: 978-1-64456-925-2 [Kindle]
ISBN: 978-1-64456-926-9 [ePub]
ISBN: 978-1-64456-927-6 [Audiobook]

Library of Congress Control Number: 2026912526

INDIES UNITED PUBLISHING HOUSE, LLC
P.O. BOX 3071
QUINCY, IL 62305-3071

INDIESUNITED.NET

"And we will call it Pacifica..."
--Nathan Green

Killionaire

The Pacifica Series

Book One

Scott Leckie

1

The lecture commenced in the now famous hall where history books had universally agreed it had all started. With her first words, Professor Trinity van Boven reminded the students that the original document from which she was about to read, although lightly frayed and partially discolored by the tropical heat, was on public display in Pacifica, safely protected by thick glass and climate controls, much like the original copies of the *US Constitution*, the *United Nations Charter* and the *Pacifica Promise*.

The unsigned document, famously made available to the Guardian newspaper on August 27, 2029, was now almost one hundred years old. Van Boven, who taught the popular graduate-level class—*PS 420 New Politics, New Planet*—always began the inaugural session of this widely over-subscribed course by reading what she felt was *the* opening salvo in the global political struggle that had brought the world to the beautiful place it is today.

She lightly cleared her throat and began to read aloud to those assembled:

> *We are out of options. We must do something, anything. The situation is now so bad that I find it difficult to unearth any words strong enough to accurately describe the daily horrors that confront us. It is out of control. Our planet is dying, our climate is changing beyond recognition, and yet, the richest among us, our human family, get richer and richer with each passing year—indeed, each passing day—while billions upon*

billions of us barely scrape by. The billionaires know all about this, but none have visited any of the world's 250,000 slums in years. None have been courageous enough to spend their money alleviating human suffering. A suffering that they largely cause.

The problem is that we are not alone on this planet. The Earth is being torn apart, driven mostly by greed—but for far too many out of need. And so, a tiny group squeezes out more wealth for the already overflowing bank accounts of the billionaire class, without even a casual thought for the damage done to our fragile world.

It is said that we need nature, but nature doesn't need us. However, the world I see today looks a lot different than that. Nature strains as forests disappear, ice melts, and methane escapes from thawed permafrost. Even space is polluted with disgusting, permanently circulating neon advertisements and millions of pieces of space junk, which the very motherfuckers who created them will never clean up.

I say it again: Our world is dying. This is not an exaggeration. This is neither melodrama nor hyperbole. This is the simple truth. The same place on which we all depend is slowly losing its ability to regenerate and repair the damage already done. And yes, the time for waiting has ended.

The time for patience is over.

The time for action is now.

We are everywhere.

Pacifica needs you!

Will you join us?

2

The call came while Jasper Eijkelje relaxed on one of his thirty teak lounge chairs, doubtlessly illegally logged from a protected forest somewhere in the tropics, most likely Myanmar, lined up in perfect rows on the front deck of his 180-meter yacht.

"Soma has set aside its best table for you tonight, sir."

"Uitstekend," he replied in Dutch, the language of his childhood, which he fell back into whenever emotions coursed through his overworked veins—one blood highway more than any other. "Tell Jaap to get the chopper ready so we can get there on time. I don't want to miss a single course. And make sure those egalitarian Danish idiots have a proper place for us to land it. I fucking hate it when we can't sit her down wherever we want."

"Ja, meneer," Iene replied. "You got it, geen probleem hoor," said his ever-ready personal assistant. Come night or day, fair weather or foul, Iene was always on call whenever Jasper needed her, evil deed or not.

As if we are all equal. How stupid can they be? he thought, conjuring up infinite images of his unique manifestation of greatness, dancing like whirling dervishes, deep inside his head.

Despite his sporty good looks and quick mind, Eijkelje was, indeed, by any measure, an *eijkelje*—the colloquial Dutch curse word for the helmet at the tip of a penis. In England he would have been called a wanker, and a supreme wanker at that. In America, he would have had to fend off the dick label. Because his name so closely resembled how he was perceived by others, he faced ruthless bullying throughout his early years. The emotional remnants from that disquieting period of his life supercharged him into becoming the horrible man he now was. He had made a thousand sad attempts to dissuade the playground bullies from name-shaming him including by changing the spelling of his name—but none of these had any impact whatsoever.

In fact, it probably made matters worse for poor little Jasper. Every time the bullies attacked him, a sadistic playground practice that started when he was only five years old, living in the middle-class Vogelenbuurt neighborhood in Utrecht on the edges of a lovely square called the Koekoeksplein, he would think, *I'll take revenge on you one day, klootzak.* Klootzak was a another genitally-related popular Dutch swearword colloquially meaning asshole but, in actual fact, referring to the little bag in which the creators of the seed that hangs so unattractively between men's legs. "You call me a penis head, and I'll call you an asshole…" Or so it went in the flatlands of the Netherlands.

As the years rolled by, after being called *Eijkelje de eijkelje* too many times to count, Jasper slowly transformed those words from a source of shame into a wellspring of power. Shame made mental room for feelings of dominance. Trauma begets trauma, and Jasper's trauma had most certainly not yet been resolved. He never tried to escape his past, but anyone who knew his story could clearly see it was very much responsible for what had transformed him into the vile creature that he had become. He was *almost* the richest person in the world, but not just yet. There was still so much damage to be done.

"The chopper's ready to roll, sir."

"OK, give me ten minutes, and then let's go."

After indulging in another of a long line of debauched cruises around the exquisite islands of the Swedish and Finnish archipelagos in June and July 2028, he had moored his ultra-mega yacht, *Ream Machine*, onto a private pier located on the outskirts of Copenhagen. When he had bought the cruise-liner-sized floating fortress from a fellow BilliBro for the paltry sum of 650 million dollars, it was originally named *Dream Machine*. On taking possession of this aquatic marvel, his first order was for Iene to hitch up a safety harness, climb down the back of the boat, and erase the letter 'D'. He then insisted that she delete the small letter 'r' and replace it with a capital 'R', rechristening the boat with its tasteless new name.

Whenever he was on the radio with local harbor authorities or a Coast Guard boat, this childish man relished saying, "*Ream Machine* here, come in, harbor master, over." He grinned a dirty smirk of a smile the whole time, always looking around to see if anyone on board had overheard him.

Now he was heading back to Holland for a few weeks of business to see how closely he could inculcate himself with a newly elected racist scoundrel who headed the country's largest political party, and to use these new relations to find more deals, make more mammon. Then he would move on to the Caribbean for several months, as a prelude to squeezing through the Panama Canal. Every time he and his crew approached the canal, he would announce through the yacht's public address system to everyone on board, "My cock is my boat, and the canal is the cunt," at which point even his most loyal of crew members would scoff and embarrassingly look down on the wooden deck feeling only shame that they had allowed themselves to work for such a disgusting man. This ghoulish creature and his servants were heading to his favorite spot—his private island in Tahiti, once owned by Marlon Brando. It was not all that far from that weird place that those acidhead radicals had just bought to create some sort a deluded dream world that Jasper had heard about through the yachties grapevine. He knew any such effort would surely fail, as previous attempts had, but if for some reason it didn't fall apart quickly enough, he knew what he needed to do to ensure its failure. He hated most people, but no group more so than acidhead radicals.

Eijkelje had made his billions by mass-producing machines that enabled humans to kill other humans more efficiently than ever before. While the ability to engage in warfare and never actually look the enemy in the eye had been a feature of warfare for ages now, he had perfected it even further and would promise potential buyers that they would never have to see the faces of their victims for there would be no face to see; it would have dissolved into a puddle of protoplasm. He was an arms manufacturer. But not just that. He was an arms designer, an arms marketeer, and, when the urge overtook him, he was also an arms user. He even had his own secret army of highly paid misfit mercenaries on call when the governments and militaries he'd already bribed failed to come through. Three words were all one needed to describe this man: weapons, violence, and greed. He loved them. He needed them. And his customers always came back for more.

Eijkelje gleefully knew that the radical leftist NGOs, which monitored the scale of global deaths from the weapons he had unleashed around the world, had just announced—via a report funded by another BilliBro—that the grim milestone of one hundred thousand dead had been surpassed. Eijkelje's guns, tanks, and especially drones had killed more than one hundred thousand people across the world, 98% of whom were civilians. *Innocent civilians.* Not a single victim had done anything to deserve the death they had suffered at the hands of evil, but suffer they had. Without exception, these poor souls were targeted by the war criminals sitting in their pods in the Nevada desert, outside Moscow, or somewhere deep in Israel's southern deserts. These associates of evil played real-life videogames with the real lives of real people, in places whose names these mad war criminals couldn't even pronounce. As a result, every drone operator, without exception, ended up with severe post-traumatic stress disorder.

Though many cured their PTSD at one of the thousands of psychedelic healing centers now functioning across the planet by ingesting MDMA, psilocybin, ketamine, and other curative compounds was beside the point. Computer keyboard mass murders from thousands of kilometers away had caused this internal mental instability and the healing centers were overbooked for months ahead of time.

Americans loved Eijkelje's guns. Israelis found them particularly useful in targeting civilian buildings in areas they illegally occupied. The seedy generals in charge of far too many other armies always danced for joy when his latest delivery arrived on their shores.

Eijkelje secretly got off on knowing his creations had killed so many of what he would interchangeably call "useless humans," "surplus people," or "oxygen stealers." But he grew increasingly fearful as more people came to recognize his face—which was rapidly becoming *the* modern face of evil, displacing dictators, autocrats and various other sickos in the process. As a result, he'd begun to spend most nights on his superyacht, believing it was safer than *terra firma*.

Nevertheless, just to be sure, he had an arsenal of weapons on board, which included one hundred of the latest laser rifles, too many drones to count, retractable artillery guns on the top deck, the bow, the stern, the port side and the starboard side, and assorted hand grenades, handguns, stun guns, tasers, lasers, and even a small handheld nuclear warhead in case things got really bad.

He had tallied up what he proudly referred to as his "fuckquests" over the eight weeks of his most recent trip. He counted forty-six Scandinavian beauties, so easily seduced and enamoured by his wealth that they let him invade their sacred zones of mystery, their jade gates to his jade peak, as the naughty Taoists might put it. They sipped ambrosian liquids scented with cloudberries, while he took them from behind on the bow of the ship, each time yelling, "I'm the king of the world!" whenever he released his load of a new strain of incurable HIV-infected sperm into their unknowing tunnels of lust. Despite repeated pleas to do so, he never wore protection, and his fuckquest journal testified to his insatiable need to overcome self-hatred with hedonistic conquests. But they could only distract him so far…

Eijkelje wasn't just about fucking blonde-haired beauties; he was out to fuck the world, and, for the moment at least, he was winning. If it meant death, disease, disharmony, and disgust, then so be it, as long as he ended up on top.

3

The soft southern California coastal breeze blew gently through Nathan Green's bouncy brown curls, just as he turned his gaze to the final page of Aldous Huxley's *Island*, a book he had already read more than a dozen times. After years of political activism, traversing the world, setting up NGOs and political movements and living out a freedom fighter's dream life, he was more certain than ever before about how he would spend the rest of his days. He would create a utopian world on an island, better than Huxley's Pala. He didn't yet know from precisely where he would coordinate the transformation of this dream into reality, but he did know for certain that it would be this to which he would dedicate the remaining time he had on Earth.

Nathan's choices—which issues to focus on, where to work, what specific tactical goals to achieve—merged together as elements of an ongoing, almost perpetual evolution that led him to always be eight steps ahead of where most others were, leading many of his contemporaries to use words like 'pioneer' or 'vanguard' to describe his interesting path. His victories were numerous and the changes that occurred because of these were far from insignificant. But, taking the same trajectory as most of his fellow humans who had also chosen career paths designed to reduce human suffering, there was no doubting that, on honest assessment, the failures vastly outnumbered the relatively rare victories. It was on a day that he was contemplating this sad yet expected truth that he again turned to Huxley for inspiration. It was time for something big.

He would prove that utopia was possible—and not just the "no place" from which the word was originally derived. From there, the word would spread, and the system and techniques he and his friends deployed to make this dream come true would become increasingly known. Hopefully, before his life ended, the entire world would transform into the utopia that an ever-growing number of people believed possible—though even more feared it never would. Every day as he arose from his overused futon, every walk he took through the fragrant fir forests, and during each and every meditation session in which he would engage, Nathan would create inner visions of just what this utopia would look like. He didn't need to look far for inspiration as Tofino and the surrounding beaches, forests, mountains and inland waterways were about as close to utopia as anyone could ever hope for. Anyone visiting Nathan and his parents for the first time would universally extol the beauties all around them and within 24 hours of arrival would use *that* word – utopia – to describe the world they were now so lucky to directly experience, rainy days or not.

Nathan was born in the early 1990s on exquisite Vancouver Island off the west coast of Canada and spent most of his youth there, living in an off-grid home near Tofino with his doting artist parents, going only occasionally to Victoria and even more rarely to Vancouver itself. In many ways it was an idyllic youth. But as happy as he was spending hours every day in the pristine forests and shorelines of the island, he knew that once he finished high school it would be time to hit the road and embrace the people of the planet. And that is precisely what he did, working as an activist, an author, a revolutionary campaigner, passionate lover and poet in lands far and wide. After more than two decades of work and travel, he was slowly coming to an acceptance that it might be time to begin some semblance of a settling down process. And so, at the tender age of forty-one after much hesitation, he decided to move to the United States from his most recent rather utopian abode in Luang Prabang, Laos. After six years in Laos, meditating in a different series of Buddhist temples every day, befriending monk after monk and merging again with a unique culture so different from his Vancouver Island home, he felt the urge to shake the light roots he had established in this spiritual tropical paradise, loosen the hold of this latest utopian domicile and replant himself somewhere else, yet again.

As he strolled down the charming lanes of Luang Prabang often passing close by the steamy banks of his beloved Mekong River, the monks with their bowls and saffron robes who knew him seemed to know before he did that he was probably more likely to depart than to stay. There was a look in his eyes, less of a jump in his stride, and a slightly gloomy sense surrounding him that the bald meditators noticed even before Nathan did so himself. They were right. It was time to leave, but where? By now, Nathan could move anywhere he wished. He could always find a way to get residency, find work either locally or internationally and because of his incomparable social skills, could develop a local friendship group within hours of arriving at his next destination. It was just a matter of choosing. His list of potential places was long. It included Cape Town in South Africa, Pondicherry in India, Santa Clara in Bolivia and Reykjavik, Iceland. After finding enough flaws in each option, the list also included a small coastal town in the country south of the border from the Canadian coastal village in which he was raised.

He moved to Orange County in California, not for the local politics, though this was changing toward the progressive. Rather, after calling more than twenty-eight nations home for various periods of time and working in almost one hundred countries, he now wanted to be as close as possible to the origins of what he saw as one of the most mysterious but utterly inspiring movements the United States had ever known. He was going to finish what the Brotherhood of Eternal Love never could. The Brotherhood were some of the first to fully embrace the unity of the human race, a perspective assisted greatly by their two favourite activities.

That crowd of blond-haired surfers from Laguna Beach, where Nathan now lived, had been the diviners of Orange Sunshine LSD in the mid-1960s, shaping the Sixties themselves as the world now defined them. Nathan would create the world's first truly psychedelic society—an elusive concept to define precisely—from which the rest of the world would follow. First, it would be the islands, and thereafter, the planet—or *Planeta Psychedelica*—as he used to like to think of it.

Legend had it, the Brotherhood—many still living—had secretly buried a million doses of a powerful acid batch in Woodland Close, the enclave where it all began, just behind the current site of the Sawdust Festival: the present location of America's most splendid annual market. The rustic and earthy paths which wound through the stalls were covered in the thick and pungent sawdust that gave this magical place its name. This hippy haven of handmade crafts was antithetical to the Laguna Beach Arts Festival and Pageant of the Masters across the road, which attracted the area's more collared shirt conservative crowd, who preferred to avoid sawdust, dirt, patchouli, and the constant waft of indica skunk weed smoke that was a permanent feature of this mini utopia. It was in this tiny enclave of Woodland Close that John Griggs and the other founders of the Brotherhood of Eternal Love had gotten their start, a minuscule part of an otherwise progressive corner of a place in the world's most powerful nation that was even more forward-looking than the majority population in a destination place to which the artists, the LGBTI+ crowd, hippies, rockers, and surfers had flocked in the 1960s and ever since.

The buried Orange Sunshine legend inspired many to move to the area over the decades. While most dismissed it as a myth from the psychedelic Sixties, the few remaining Brotherhood members swore it was true. After years of heavy LSD use, none of them were interested in tripping anymore themselves as they entered their eighties. Instead, it became a matter of honor to keep the location of the elusive Lysergic Holy Grail a secret.

It was widely believed that Augustus Owsley Stanley III, the so-called Northern California competitor—as the capitalists would put it—had done the same in the upper half of the same state and maybe in Australia, as well, though competition was hardly a factor in the world of the trippers. As the producer of millions more doses of this magical elixir, his actions were often compared to those of the Brotherhood. Owsley moved to northeast Australia early in the acid revolution, and legend claimed he had buried one hundred million hits of his strongest batch (way too strong for ordinary mortals, in fact) near the upscale town of Port Douglas in Queensland, where he lived off the land in the Daintree Rainforest. Almost sixty years later, no one had ever found it, and though stories about the missing acid would occasionally pop up on Australia's mass media, its location, too, remained a mystery.

Nathan Green planned to achieve what the Brotherhood sought but failed to do. He would somehow seek to acquire an island and then loosely follow Huxley's *Island* as a blueprint for his utopia. He would make it happen, come what may. Yes, it would cost a fair amount, but he knew some seriously wealthy people who might help. Even then, so much of utopia didn't require money at all, let alone the exploitation of Nature. Rather, he knew that it was Nature itself that held all the answers—or at least the most important ones. Sure, there would be technology, but they would start by using no fossil fuels and carrying out world-leading research on renewables. They would first use and test these technologies, then sell them to the rest of the world, providing cleaner air and cooling temperatures while generating the funds to spread the vision of Pacifica beyond the palm-fringed shores of the still unknown mystical island.

Green was accustomed to being the target of vitriol for his visionary ideas, especially from the BilliBros, most of whom had never so much as seen LSD or mushrooms, despite Steve Jobs's frequent praise of LSD as one of the most profound experiences of his life. If lanky Steve couldn't convince them, no one could. But Nathan knew that those BilliBros – more than anyone - needed a dose, a huge dose. On the rare occasions when the world's 0.00003% courageously took the plunge, the inherent and awful weirdness of the BilliBro world seemed to slip away into oblivion. All the things that they had once deemed so invaluable, especially having a net worth higher than the next guy, faded away into realms of the unbelievable. Some of them went to Burning Man to have a small taste, though most would have never even contemplated visiting such scenes of free love, drugs, and debauchery.

But sometimes, they did muster up the courage to explore the inner recesses of their minds; and when they did, extraordinary things became possible. One rather famous BilliBro was once, in between uncontrollable bouts of alternating weeping and attendant relief, heard to say, "How could I have been so shallow?" as he emerged from his five grams of *Stropharia cubensis* mushroom trip back into the reality he was used to but with a wholly different worldview. Instead of competition, envy, fear, hatred, and exploitations, he embraced love, kindness, unity, and compassion. Some of them even extolled sympathy and giving, happily handing over billions to worthy causes everywhere.

In the mushroom-induced, limitless void, the lucky ingestors finally *got* the obscenity of even the "poorest" billionaires holding over 133,000 times the median global net worth, while the richest held thirty-two million times more. "How is this even allowed?" "How was this even possible?" they often wondered with a collective sneer on their three thousand faces. "How can governments be so afraid of us that they continue to fail to act against us?" It was a big jump, that is for sure. It was a leap that one makes just once in a lifetime, but that once was more than what was needed to shake things into the place and get them to where they belonged. The problem was, of course, that only a tiny handful of the younger BilliBros ever engaged with these life-altering substances. Not more than 1% of them would ever even contemplate it.

What an entirely different world we would have if those cowardly BilliBros were more keen to delve into the Limitless Void, thought Nathan on an hourly basis.

Nathan knew that Earthlings had more than enough resources on the planet to turn this unique outpost into the utopia he envisioned, rather than the hellhole run by the lowest levels of human consciousness that it became as more and more wealth—from the exploited world in the Global South—flowed straight into the secret bank accounts of the billionaires. He also believed that if he could get more of the BilliBros to see the proverbial light, Earth and its people might still stand a chance.

And that's when Amber entered his life.

4

Nathan grabbed another glass of cannabis-infused kombucha early in the evening on what would surely be an all-night rowdy fiesta, well before the intoxicants went to work, and strolled straight back to the always-smiling Amber, the nicest woman he had ever met at a party. They had met for the first time less than an hour earlier, and now it was as if an invisible forcefield was holding them together, powered by a form of destiny beyond definition. They were feeling it. There was no possible way to control it. They let it overwhelm then like a 12-foot wave shaped like a perfect barrel ready to be surfed by anyone lucky enough to be nearby. It was chemical. Although he could have seduced any woman anywhere, and plenty of dudes, too, rarely had things gotten so overheated so quickly. He and Amber were into it, and after one more kombucha, they stepped outside into the destiny-laden Laguna Beach air and quickly spotted their Uber.

"So, where do you want to go, cutie?" she asked.

Even ever-so-desirable Nathan was taken aback by her forwardness and hesitated for a moment before attempting a reasonable retort to her tantalizing query.

"Well, we could go to my pad over in Woodland Close, but it's a bit of a mess. I've been researching my next book, and there's paper everywhere, books all over the place, and I hate to tell you that I haven't done the dishes for at least a week, I haven't vacuumed for a month or more and probably haven't dusted for at least a year. This book has been all-consuming, and everything else comes second these days, except for you, my new friend Amber."

She beamed a blushing-face-smile, wondering if she would ever set foot in Woodland Close herself, and giggled. "OK, let's go to my place."

The kind blond-haired driver asked where he should go, and Amber softly indicated her wish to go up the hill to the Mountain Mead Estate.

"Mountain Mead Estate? That sounds like something you'd find in upstate New York or some such place. I was always curious why they named it that way," Nathan pondered out loud. Then he remembered that the estate was where the richest of the rich, the elitist of the elite, lived, though he had never been there before. "You mean that place on the hill where the billionaires live? You live there, Amber? No way! Do you work for one of the BilliBros? Are you a maid or a cleaner or something?"

Amber smiled and somewhat guiltily said, "Yes, I must admit I still live with my parents in a little cottage on the grounds of our compound. I do all my paintings there, and they pretty much leave me alone. They're not here much, anyway. They seem to like the Hamptons house more. And, yes, just to get it out of the way, in case you are wondering, I *am* a trust fund baby, but I promise you this didn't mess me up, like all those others you see on that *SuperMe* App and those dismal TV shows. I despise them and can tell you from first-hand experience they are universally horrible humans. Over the years, for some idiotic reason, I have stupidly gone on vacation with more than one of those nitwits."

She shook her head. "Once I went to St. Barts with the daughter of a 'beverage magnate,' as he likes to call himself… whatever the hell that means. I went to Cannes with the family of a perfume heiress and even—how could I have done this? —went gazelle hunting with some animal-killing creep who calls himself John Jr., who is truly one of the vilest humans alive. Far worse than even his disgusting, pussy-grabbing, criminal, dictator-wannabe father. I actually vomited all over him after he tried to kiss me, the smell of it mixing with the blood of the lion he had just illegally killed. It was awful. I hate all of them. I know I'm one of them, but I don't feel like I am. I hope I'm not tainted beyond redemption! I can't wait to get full control over my fund next month when I turn thirty. Then I'll be out of there and use the cash to be surrounded by truly kind, generous, and loving people instead of all the fuckwits who encircle me now."

Nathan listened as closely as he could, correctly believing himself to be the luckiest man alive. He had had many girlfriends, had travelled the world and met thousands upon thousands of phenomenal women from every continent. He knew the planet and knew humanity, but he had never known a spontaneous love like this. A quality of destiny surrounded her, filling the space with bright light, as if blissful explosions of joy went off whenever she appeared. And it seemed quite obvious that she felt the same about him. It was undoubtedly written in the stars, meant to be, and had to be—their lives, and perhaps the entire human race, depended on it.

Amber finally stopped talking and, with her make-up-free face, looked more closely at her party conquest. Then glanced at the driver as she waited for a reply, but none came.

Nathan was stunned into silence as he suddenly realized he was in an Uber with none other than the daughter of Harry Fucking Prescott Fucking Ness! He couldn't believe it. Though appalled by the realization, he felt the tingling of an idea that, not all that long in the future, he would recognize as crucial for ending the worst excesses of the scourge of inequality brought about by the neo-liberal era dominating the planet since that evil duo—Ronnie-Ray-gun and Maggie-the-Milk-Snatcher—unleashed the tiger and the injustices that, unhindered, would bring the world to the edge of oblivion.

He gathered his thoughts and, using every ounce of energy he could muster in his shocked state, said, "Wow, I've never been to Mountain Mead Estates. I can't wait." Trying to sound wealthy, he added, "I hope you have some good Veuve Clicquot up there."

"Sure do, cutie. What do you take me for, a peasant?"

5

Nathan knew more than most that all humans were, at their core, the same. He had criss-crossed the planet enough to know this truth at the depths of his soul. With this awareness came an almost withering sense of empathy for each and every fellow human leading him to waver between thoughts of immense compassion towards those responsible for the suffering of most of humanity and the deepest possible levels of scorn for this very same group of evil-doers. What Nathan hated most about his uncontrollable yin-yang personality was being inexorably pulled from his peaceful role as a selfless sage and extolling wisdom-giver into the role of a mad scientist. Despite his pure and socially minded motives, this job involved a series of rather serious crimes that greatly infringed on the rights of those affected.

Yes, of course, the victims had committed far worse crimes on far larger numbers of people, for a far longer period, but still… He had realized long ago that it would take active non-compliance with the law and the removal of certain strategically selected individual freedoms to move the world in a direction where it could continue to exist at all. “A small price to pay,” he opined to only himself.

There’s a reason groups like Extinction Rebellion spring up every so often, he thought.

If he was to do something dramatic, it would have to be clearly done in the interests of humanity. It needed to be so pure in intention, yet so daring in execution, that most of the world would support him if he got into too much trouble. The plan he had in mind would do just that. Indeed, it needed to be so good and flawlessly executed that if anyone ever tried to bring him to justice, he knew a mere snap of his fingers could mobilize billions of people on the streets.

Take that billionaires, he thought to himself. *You call that power. That's not power, THIS is power*, he thought as he acted out the famous knife scene from the film "Crocodile Dundee."

Then he'd switch back into what he referred to as his 3M self—mellow man mode—imparting titbits of deep philosophical insights to anyone willing to listen, which, admittedly, was no small number.

When you choose, you lose, he ruminated yet again. His push-and-pull personality grated on him, so he began contemplating an exit strategy that minimized blame on him while maximizing the success of his Earth-saving plan, which lay on the northern side of high. The latter, of course, mattered to him far more than he could ever imagine. If authorities caught him and, against all odds, the masses failed in their quest to free him, he wouldn't mind spending a few years behind bars. Not only would he be forced to meditate even more than he already did, but he could sit there in peace, knowing that he had truly changed the world for the better—and in ways that were staggering for all to see.

His ideas would spread like a positive virus, an empathy virus, seeping into every mind—past, present, and future. His insights revealed that life was about much more than the four hundred generations before him had ever realized. His vision combined insights from Amazonian root brews, 1960s hippie philosophies, Tibetan wisdom from Himalayan caves, ancient Egyptian knowledge, and other wonders of the world into a psychedelic vision for a planet without greed. But there was even more to it than just that.

He had somehow discovered a musical groove that was always there but never played. A melodic song line that had yet to be sung by any living being. It was a sound never before heard. It came from a giant, beautifully stained one-stringed Kosmic bass that, when plucked by a single finger, let out a tone, a hum, a vibration that shook the collective DNA of every living thing. It sent shivers of eternal joy down the spines of roosters and pine trees, humans and roadside weeds, and heck, even within the sagging scrota and decaying ovaries of billionaires worldwide.

The magic of these new sounds was nothing short of epic, not only for their life-saving dimensions but for how they comprehensively transformed worldviews almost *in toto*. Of course, people still needed the basics: water, food, shelter, community, tender loving care, and the occasional intense orgasm.

Largely gone, however, would be the endless grasping, relentless search for more, mass consumption, morbid obesity, mindless fossil-fuel-burning, fear, paranoia, us-versus-them attitudes, power quests, torture, killing, war build-up, domestic violence, and income inequality—all built on the dreadfully low-level minds on the pyramid of consciousness scale that had been normalized, and ruled the world since the dawn of the Industrial Age, an era of progress that had ultimately begun to devour its creators, the human race.

The Anthropocene had arrived without a moment's notice and was unlikely to ever be reversed.

At least we could control it in a good way, or so Nathan thought. Since humans have altered the world beyond recognition—causing mass extinctions, devastating climate change, rising sea levels, clear-cutting forests, and destroying oceans—why not harness these evil, destructive forces and turn it all around? Much like an Aikido master who uses an opponent's violent energy against them—turning a vicious left hook, right uppercut, or swinging kick to the kidneys right back at the unprincipled, uncaring foe—why not redirect these forces to address the damage and correct the course?

"We could be like that." Nathan opined.

And so, as black cannot exist without white, nor bad without good, nor many without none, Mr. So Sure of Himself, But Also Ever So Doubtful—the Prince of Paradox—continued on his merry way along the beaches of Laguna and the laneways of Woodland Close, a magic mushroom never far from his awaiting tongue, planning to end the billionaire-powered world and transform it into something far better and more desirable, ushering in an unprecedented era—an epoch, in fact—unlike the world had ever known. This would be the true end of history, not because unbridled capitalism had won, but, in fact, because it had lost. All thanks to Nathan and his merry friends, the long-haired pretty boy—so impatient to remove dear Amber's purple thong—feared his own firm, strong, and bulging testicle container might, too, one day become one of those sagging scrota that the BilliBros so famously dragged around the world in their private planes and rocket ships. But he wasn't about to let thoughts of an unknown future get in his way. "Amber, may I please remove your lovely purple thong?"

"Of course, you god you. You can even rip it off if you'd like. I have hundreds more. Daddy buys them for me."

"What?" replied Nathan suspiciously.

"Yes, I know it's weird, but it's the truth. In fact, it's all too close to that grotesque friend of his who somehow managed to get elected president some years ago. I still can't believe America idiotically elected that fucker, who spoke about his own daughter as if she were his sex kitten, saying things like, 'If she weren't my daughter, I'd date her,' and even commented on her body and stuff. I'm done with these fucking creeps. Makes me want to vomit. In fact, I fucking hate all of them, Nathan. I hate my dad, too. They have fucked over the world, and I am done. I can tell that you want to do something about it too. I know we've just met, but I want you to know I'll do anything to help you. And when I say anything, I mean it. *Anything*. I hate money, my love, so I am going to give it all away to you. Take me, I'm yours, money and all."

And with that, the dream that had swirled with increasing vigor in this beautiful man's gorgeous mind fell into place like atoms around a nucleus.

All he said was, "And it shall be called Pacifica."

"Well, then," she said, "*Viva Pacifica Viva*!"

Off came the purple thong, never to be worn again…

6

The University of California at Irvine (UCI) wasn't always known as a bastion of leftist thought, but radical students like Jason Mooi could always find some exceptionally progressive professors if they looked carefully enough. Jason eagerly anticipated his next class; he always arrived early to the lecture hall, a place that would one day be seen to hold as much significance as Versailles, Yalta or Independence Hall not just to a few who knew their local histories, but to the entire planet. If anyone needed to find him, he'd always be in the front row, centered as close as possible to the genius teaching his favorite course, *Capitalism's Promise: Inequality, Poverty, and Decline – What Next?*

But today, there was going to be a guest speaker, the renowned French economics professor Ron Fencie. Fencie's unexpected 2012 best seller, *Wealth Always Beats Work*, as dry as it may seem from the title, had changed Jason's life irreparably and led to what became his lifelong quest to bring equality back into fashion. He couldn't wait to see Fencie speak and had a whole series of questions lined up to ask his hero at the end of the crowded evening event.

When Fencie arrived at the lectern, Jason felt like a music fan anticipating the moment his favorite band took the stage. After hearing a kind introduction from his open-minded professor and quickly averting the beginnings of a fainting spell when he realized he was only three meters away from Fencie, Jason leaned in as the French intellectual began to speak.

"Ow many of you, 'ave read my book *Always*, my friends?" Fencie began his speech, displaying a French accent as wonderful to the ear as an inimitable croissant was on their taste buds. Quite literally everyone in the audience raised their hands.

Fencie pretended to make a gesture as if he was leaving the stage, hiding his face in mock embarrassment. Everyone laughed, and he simply said, "Well, then you really only need to remember one small number from my tome, and that, of course, is thirty-eight million US dollars. Yes, thirty-eight million. Remember that number, my friends." He famously used his sharp mind and strong moral compass to argue that a fair global economic system—one that preserved the environment and protected the rights of everyone, everywhere—would only be possible if no one could amass more than thirty-eight million dollars in net worth. Anyone who earned or possessed any amount of money that surpassed that hefty sum would simply be taxed at 100%, so the thirty-eight-million-dollar threshold could never be exceeded. The tiny proportion of humanity reaching that level could still have their yachts, fly first class, routinely eat their caviar and truffles, and own multiple homes, but the days of grotesque inequality borne from neo-liberal economics would end. But how would that come to be?

The question had a very easy set of answers. Great minds like Robert Reich, Vandana Shiva, Rutger Bregman, and Yuval Noah Harari could pinpoint the exact moments when decisions in the corridors of power unleashed market forces, backed by beholden politicians, that had created today's billionaire-dominated world. Other great minds, like those of Fencie and Green, prepared to do something about it—and soon, they would. How desperately Jason hoped to be able to join them.

The economic and political power of the billionaire class was grotesque and continued to grow with each passing year as government after government refused to take the obvious measures needed to reign them in. The markets were booming, and so too were the portfolios of the BilliBros. Ordinary taxpayers in the wealthier countries were used to paying anywhere between 25-50% of their incomes as tax, but, on average, the BilliBros of the planet were paying less than 3% of their incomes in tax. The world was increasingly becoming a sort of *anything goes* structure that allowed and enabled the most powerful to get away with anything they wanted. They would each hang an invisible, but very real, Sword of Damocles above the collective heads of governments everywhere, always with the implicit threat that should a government put in place measures designed to fairly tax billionaires, close the loopholes and ban offshore accounts, the billionaires would simply shift their assets away and follow shortly thereafter with their investments, factories and everything else. Until now, these threats of flight were more than sufficient to keep any real measures against the billionaires at bay. When even very soft murmurs arose that a government was planning to impose a minimum tax on billionaires, or that asset freezes might be put into place until such taxes were paid, the global billionaire class banded together almost instantaneously and made it very clear that if governments wanted to keep benefitting from their riches, they had better leave them be.

It was sentiments and actions such as these that had helped Fencie's ideas to gain as much traction as they already had. People across the world were slowly awaking to the evils of billionairism and were tiring of it. These billionaires were just people, as they were people. How an average person anywhere could have just a few thousand dollars to their name and a group of 3,000 people, physiologically identical to them, had more than one billion dollars each was inexplicable. It was shocking and it was wrong. It was time to start discussing the idea of limits. If the world failed in this quest, before too long there would not merely be billionaires on planet Earth with disproportionate power over almost everything and everyone, but there would be *trillionaires*. Yes, the existence of trillionaires was the next logical outcome of governments failing to enact laws and policies to induce equality.

Once the idea of wealth limits had fully settled into the minds of those assembled, the crowd cheered as if the Beatles had just entered the stage in 1964, and an impromptu and extremely loud chant of "thir-tee-eight, thir-tee-eight, thir-tee-eight" emerged from the energized audience—so loud that people could feel there was a lot of conviction behind that number.

Fencie was accustomed to applause, but this was something new.

Never before had he heard such untethered enthusiasm from a crowd. But as it continued, he noticed something that began to worry him. The positive chanting was evolving into something else entirely; it was now infused with a tinge of anger, a tingle of hatred, and even the smatterings of possible violence. He tried to calm them down, raised his hands, smiled, and used all the other techniques public speakers practice to mellow things out. Slowly the dynamism of the shouting began to fade.

As the decibels dropped a notch, he noticed one person in the crowd who wasn't flailing in rage against the BilliBros who were wantonly destroying the world. A calm young man, his hair falling far below his shoulders, sat in subdued glee, barely smiling. Unlike the others, he didn't gesticulate, knowing it was he who had breathed life into the local community's engagement with the growing global movement against the 0.00003%. He knew the world's future was on the brink, and disaster loomed ever closer.

Change was coming, and Jason knew it. Change was coming, and Jason was about to foment it.

And then, as if driven by an uncontrollable force—which even he could not derive the origins of—Jason jumped out of his seat and yelled at the top of his lungs, his voice quivering, "Let's block the fucking entrance to the hill where the BilliBros live! And either keep 'em in or keep 'em from fucking things up more—or keep 'em out and make 'em nervous!"

The unruly crowd erupted in cheers, quickly turning into a unified chant: "Block that road! Block that road!"

Someone with years of demonstrating experience began a call-and-response rallying cry with, "What do we want?" And then the crowd, not really knowing what to say, precisely, went quiet for a moment until someone shouted out, "Blockade!"

"What do we want?" "Blockade!"

"When do we want it?" "Now!"

Over and over again. After about fifty cycles of call and response, with the room bursting with energy, Jason led the crowd out of the hall and onto the streets, marching toward the hill just a couple of kilometers away. Without a permit or a plan, and with no clear idea of what would happen, everyone felt that something had to be done, and if not by them, then by whom?

They haphazardly hopped into an armada of vehicles for the quick but wholly unplanned ride up the hill and marched for five more minutes to the outer gate of the wealthy's fortress containing smaller fortresses. There, they sat down in unison in the middle of the road—young and old, of all genders, income groups, religions, and races—fifty people thick, hundreds strong, blocking the road in rows so no car could pass.

The armed guards at the gate, this being America—the most gun-obsessed culture in the world—became perturbed by the roadblock, viewing it as a criminal act, an intentionally illegal act, despite the demonstrators' non-threatening presence. As they prepared to call for reinforcements, a car pulled up next to the throng. Fencie, rolling down the window, hoped to calm the crowd and redirect them to a less obstructive spot and gain better media attention. But seeing the crowd's size and conviction, instead of looking for leaders like Jason, he couldn't suppress the beginnings of a smile. He realized that while the past, aborted movements—Occupy, 99%, Black Lives Matter, the Yellow Vests of France—had been impactful, they had fizzled out quickly without achieving lasting structural change. But now, right here and now, it felt different. Very different. There was a clear aim: the very end of billionairism itself. There was a clear target: the billionaires. And there was a clear pathway to achieve this: the thirty-eight-million rule and all that that implied.

Added to this, it had been clear for years now that the world was desperate for a new way of doing things. A new economic and political system based on the Earth and the human family, all set within and entirely dependent upon the very same ecosystem: the truth of Gaia. There had been countless attempts to make this happen, but somehow, it had never come to be. The forces of nationalism, dictatorship, and disunity proved no match for visions of greater equality, more sustainable economic systems, and rights for everyone. Billions of people wanted a more compassionate world, a more peaceful world. They wanted the planet to merge closer and closer, where no one felt superior or more deserving than anyone else but achieving this had proved elusive. People were tired of Planet Hate. They wanted Planet Love. And if the Killionaire had their way, this would be precisely what they would get.

At that moment, Fencie knew it was time. He knew this was it. It would happen now. Instead of urging the crowd to move, he smiled and yelled, "Do not stop, ever! We must end the existence of billionaires now! They are killing our countries. They are eroding democracy. They hide their assets in tax havens. They destroy the natural environment. They are a criminal class and they must go away forever!" Then, he rolled up the window and told the driver to head to the airport for the next flight to the next town, where he would deliver the same message, which would always culminate with the number thirty-eight.

7

The fact that the crowd kept chanting "thir-tee-eight, thir-tee-eight, thir-tee-eight…" with increasing vigor stuck in his mind, worrying not only Fencie but Jason too. Jason was happy to have sparked the growing awareness of the new numerical deity, the Almighty Thirty-Eight, but couldn't help feeling uncomfortable that it might become so popular that things might get out of hand. For a while now—many months in fact—he had noticed polite conversations turning into vicious yelling matches between those who believed billionaires were vital for innovation and economic growth and the more insightful ones, who recognized the immense dangers of this tiny sliver of humanity holding so much power over everything that ordinary people held dear, and actively undermining democracy and human rights in the process.

No matter anyone's stance on the matter, it was indisputable that the news was getting out. Just about everyone thought that the billionaires controlled too much in too many places, causing widespread harm. They pushed the planet's limits to the point where life itself was threatened, especially human life. "If this isn't a disease, then what is?" Jason thought. The fact that just three thousand humans could bring the entire human race so close to perpetual oblivion astounded even the most aware, who knew that eradication of the billionaire class was the only way forward.

The political classes, who had allowed this odious cancer to grow and flourish without a single dose of chemo or radiation to nip it in the bud, increasingly realized that they had to act or risk falling out of favor with the BilliBros—as if these rich lunatics were the sole group with any true power.

Jason realized full well that very few people adequately understood the BilliBro scourge because ordinary people struggled to conceptualize just how abominably rich a billionaire was in contrast to a mere mortal human being. Citizens understood that billionaires could buy anything, anytime, and anywhere. They understood that they often had a disproportionately high number of children. They knew they had multiple homes, boats, planes, bank accounts, and all the rest. These were all things people could understand in material terms, even though virtually no one could ever dream of acquiring such immense wealth.

But it was the gargantuan degree of inequality that confused people the most. They simply couldn't mentally conceive that a single person could possess hundreds of thousands or even millions of times more wealth than the average person. How was this even possible, let alone allowed? Jason developed graphics that depicted the scale of these differences, but while these were shocking, they still did not seem sufficient to allow ordinary citizens to have the mental break through required to truly grasp the utter absurdity of billionairism. Knowing that the BilliBros held more than fifteen trillion US dollars of wealth between them was just a number, although a very true one. Its actual size was almost impossible to understand and so, without adequate intervention by governments or the markets, the billionaires continued to grow in number.

Jason calculated that the wealth ratio of the poorest billionaire (one billion and one dollar) compared to the average global person was like Usain Bolt running one hundred meters in 9.58 seconds, while the average person took over fourteen days to travel the same distance. He found out that if an average person is 160cm tall, the billionaire would be more than 220 kilometers tall. If the average person weighed 70kgs, the billionaire would weigh the same as fifty-eight Blue Whales. Unfortunately, even these extraordinary figures proved incapable of swaying the population. Clearly, Jason's work would be cut out for him.

Some clever international activists had delved deeply into many of the BilliBro secrets and exposed them on a grand scale and this did begin having an impact. Banking secrecy had been exposed. The secret law firms that coordinated the creation of offshore companies and accounts were now known. Global wealth taxes were proposed and measures to stop large-scale tax evasion were making small strides, but a great distance remained. Despite small steps forward in the world's richest country, American billionaires paid an average of 3.4% tax on their income, revealing who truly held power in what was still remarkably called a "democracy," even though it stopped being a functioning democracy many years before.

Jason noticed that the key US adversary, China, began creating billionaires at nearly the same rate as the US, so in the end this was never at all a battle between the right or the left positions on the political spectrum. Most new Chinese billionaires continued on their merry way, but several of the flashier, media-savvy billionaires in China soon faced harassment from the government and disappeared from public view. Jason's first thought upon learning of these crackdowns, was: *When China seems to be doing the right thing, the world truly has a major problem on its hands.* This applied to finance and social class, but even more so to politics, where terms like "dictator," "killer," "torturer," or "glutton" could be easily interchanged with "billionaire." In a world where accessing billions frequently involved politics, these roles were interchangeable.

As ripples of these obvious facts reached elected parliaments and other decision-makers, Jason and his friends began to have a glimmer of hope—that something, *anything* would be done—to better equalize the world's financial affairs in favor of the people as a whole in contrast to the tiny elite at the top of the global financial pyramid.

For once, the BilliBros started getting nervous, striking back with increased venom as each proposal for reigning them in was made. Slowly but surely, governments were beginning to put an end to the absurdity of tax havens and secret numbered bank accounts. But this was never easy. Territories that depended on allowing the world's wealthiest to hide their fortunes were obviously reluctant to reject banking secrecy for the sake of transparency and other minor matters such as the survival of the planet and its people.

Bermuda decided once and for all to close all the loopholes and shutter the secret banks. It publicly declared itself a holiday haven instead of a tax haven for miscreants, full of quaint alleyways, colorful buildings, temperate weather, and some of the best whale watching anywhere. Great vibes too.

Even Singapore and Switzerland, so long associated with briefcases stuffed with ill-gotten cash, private planes, and secret stash spots for dirty money saw the writing on the wall and changed their banking secrecy laws, drip by drip. They rebuilt their economies on their reputations as clean, safe, and well-run places where people could enjoy themselves without the prospect of a seedy billionaire puffing cigars in a non-smoking restaurant unless one ghoulishly paid extra to do so, regardless of the impact on other guests.

When people like Jason, Nathan, and Amber and others who actually cared about the Earth delved deeper into these about-faces, they quickly realized they were more cosmetic than substantial. Surprise, surprise. While the changes might have impacted the planet's mere millionaires, they had no effect on the kings of the financial mountain. Some banks simply upped the ante, raising the minimum balance required to keep money with them, even if the funds were legitimate and taxed. Banks that once deployed privacy as an attractive device increased minimum balances and demanded five, ten, or twenty million, pushing out the "little guys" and reserving their services for the richest—with privacy and secrecy still very much intact. Other banks in other countries demanded public registries of beneficial ownership, indicating who owned the accounts they held, but the rich simply transferred their billions into shell companies whose names appeared on the registries, with no way to trace who actually owned the company concerned. They had it all figured out. They had already won, and now they were winning again.

Few of the BilliBros changed anything about how they lived, even as they became increasingly aware of the damage they were doing. They might have bought an electric vehicle occasionally, but they kept their obscene flashy cars, continuing to drive them to their favorite places, often paying impoverished but well-dressed parking valets five thousand bucks to keep their cars idling at the front door of the

Michelin-three-star restaurant of their choosing while they dined within.

Occasionally, Jason would cycle by such places, stop his bike, and watch as people climbed, often with difficulty, into their million-dollar cars, then revved up long before they spun out of the parking lot. It was abundantly clear to Jason—and anyone else who had encountered the BilliBros—that those with the world's biggest bank accounts were nothing special. At one level, as people, they were just people. On the other, they were as unexceptional as could be. Some of them had achieved financial super-hero success through original thinking and deep innovation, but most simply happened to be in the right place at the right time, possessing no particular skill or powerful insight. All were greedy, but only a few could truly be classified by any objective measure as anything even close to genius levels of intelligence. The bottom line: most of them were simply lucky—lucky by chance, lucky by deception, or lucky by birth.

Seeing just how pathological they were, Jason gives them a very convincing evil eye and thinks to himself, *Your days are numbered, motherfuckers. Enjoy them while you can, you dickheads.* Such sentiments did not really match gentle Jason's kind public persona; everyone knew that he instinctively loved everyone and was loved by everyone in return. Everyone, that is, except for the BilliBros who were beginning to run scared.

8

As he entered the grounds of *Winner* for the first time, Nathan suspected someone had spiked his pot kombucha with more than just hydroponic skunk weed. Though it was dark outside, even on this moonless night he could see enough that he thought he must be hallucinating. He had rubbed shoulders a few times with the wealthy but had seen nothing quite like this.

The main house resembled a castle more than a family dwelling. The pool was Olympic-sized, the two helipads covered more land than a normal suburban quarter-acre block, and the driveway was long enough for a plane to land. This was both shocking and pleasing: shocking due to the ostentation and pleasing because he knew an all-night love-making session with Amber was just around the corner. From the first kiss of the evening—which had destiny written all over it—they had both known they would be together forever. As different as their backgrounds, bank accounts, or breathless moaning might be, Nathan and Amber had no other choice than eternity, and eternity it would be. There would be no turning back, ever.

Amber led Nathan, the lustful lad, through a forest of ancient pine trees, the smell of which instantly reminded him of his island origins. They wandered past manicured rhododendrons—purple flowers still visible—to her "cottage," which had twelve rooms, sixteen-foot ceilings—with floor-to-ceiling windows—two kitchens, a sauna, hot tub, massage room, and more. Designed by Amber herself with haybales and hand-smoothed adobe walls, it was as beautiful as she was, inside and out. Yes, Amber, a twenty-nine-year-old heiress to the Ness fortune, was beautiful, vivacious, brilliant, and compassionate—the last of these four qualities which her father dismissed as "feelings of a loser." Despite this, she remained true to herself. Soon to be the beloved of a long-haired eco-warrior—a meditating oneness man, a cool cat, joint-smoking, acid-dropping, and mushroom-munching man of mindfulness—Amber walked them home through the trees. She had named each one, recognizing their unique personalities and the millions of miles of mycelia pathways beneath the soil that linked them all.

On the first day of their mind, body, and soul merger—along with the sharing of life's vital bodily fluids—dear Nathan had it in his head that he would introduce his new love to the wonders of his dreams. Little did he know, voluptuous Amber was already far ahead of him. She was always suspicious, not quick to trust anyone, including those who seemed to love her so quickly. But for both of them, it was clearly different this time. This was meant to be, pre-destined. It just had to happen. It was fate, inexplicable, raw, real, eternal.

They both lay silent for an hour in an afterglow unmatched in either of their lives, sparks of invisible energy flowing through both of them, as if a river bursting its banks unsure where to go. As things settled and Nathan reluctantly prepared to leave *Winner*, he and his new love heard frenzied shouts and chants from beyond the estate gates. The chanting took on a rhythmic nature, with drumbeats and other sounds getting louder and louder by the minute. The closer they listened, the more they perceived; and at one point, they put it all together when they heard, "What do we want?" "Blockade!" When do we want it?" "Now!"

At that moment, the Ness residence received a phone call, and, since her parents were at the Hamptons' house, Amber decided to answer. Julio at the gate informed her that a protest was blocking the road and it would likely be some time before it was cleared.

"What kind of demonstration is it, Julio?" she asked.

"Something about billionaires ruining the world and all that sort of thing; the same as always."

Instead of being afraid, Amber was overjoyed. She immediately told Nathan what she knew, then said, "Nathan, let's walk down to the gate and check it out. We might know someone in the crowd."

They walked down the perfectly manicured paths through the immaculate forest toward the front gate and, through the slats of the fence, saw none other than Nathan's best friend, Jason.

Seeing Nathan and Amber smiling, Jason laughed as he greeted his soul brother through the gate but felt anguished when he realized Amber's identity. Within an instant, it all became crystal clear, and Jason's competing smile turned quickly upside down. The pangs of jealousy entered his being like an alien force, all-encompassing, all-powerful, and all-awful when it dawned on him that this Amber was the goddess whom he had already begun calling his own. This was going to be painful, but at the same time, and much more importantly, this was too good to be contemplated.

Jason had spotted Amber around town ever since he arrived in Southern California several years earlier. Recently, he had finally generated the courage to actually speak to her the last time he saw her at Bliss Nodules Café on the Balboa Peninsula, known to be her favorite.

As she had sat there with her guard discreetly sitting on the far side of the almost painfully hip and organic café, wellness and gratitude signs everywhere one looked, Jason had spotted his chance. He quickly finished his vegan sandwich, pushed his chair away from the handmade table bought years ago at the Sawdust Festival with a small bit of cash and a large bit of weed, and strode, head up, shoulders back, yet mellow, toward the rich woman sitting a few tables away. He looked down, saw her portobello mushroom dish with just one bite remaining, and simply said, "Well, that looks good. Looks like you enjoyed it greatly."

She didn't mind being bothered if the good soul bothering her was indeed a good soul, which they mostly were not, but when they were, she actually enjoyed it. She—like all ultra-wealthy people—was universally suspicious of any new person, fearing (mostly rightfully) that they only wanted contact as a first step in some method of shaking a few million loose by any means possible. She smiled immediately after listening to Jason's words and, seeing what a nice man he was, just said, "I sure did—it was great. These guys at Nodule sure do know how to cook. Have you ever had the tempeh with the vegan aioli? It's incredible."

He was so thrilled that she didn't shoo him away that, rarely for him, he was completely dumbfounded, reduced to a mumbling radster, giggling and chortling. He then felt deeply anguished that he couldn't turn his feelings into words. When he finally settled down, she smiled again—very used to such responses from her exquisite use of language—and asked him to join her. He sat down immediately, her guard wary but not overly. After he got comfortable, she said, "So, who are you, and what do you care about?"

He smiled. "Jason, I'm Jason. What do I care about? Well, I care about equality. I want the world to be more equal. I want the better world to be for everyone, everywhere, not just a few."

He knew all too well who he was talking to. His upfront, truthful answer was risky—the kind that could make or break everything. She would either walk away, seeing him as a scoundrel, or be endeared to him forever. It was the latter. Though she fell in love with him at that moment, it was a love rooted in their shared vision of a better world, not a romantic one. She wasn't closed to the idea of amorous love, but she knew the time wasn't right for her yet. That would have to wait a while.

Jason, however, read the tea leaves differently and fell deeply and romantically in love with her at that moment. He began planning his life accordingly, despite knowing—during rare moments of rationality—that such a union would likely remain a dream. And though he was reluctant to accept this, somehow at least a small part of him did so, but only a small part.

Now, seeing her and Nathan together behind the gate, and the translucent halo-like energy that seemed to surround them, he knew his special days with Amber had come to an abrupt and unanticipated end.

9

One day later, after the noisy crowd had peacefully dispersed, one of the world's richest men was again at a loss. Reclining on his overstuffed white sofa, safely ensconced within the walls of his fourth favorite home at which he had just arrived that morning, he had no idea how to talk to or even relate to his daughter, so the only thing Ness could think to say to her was, "How many followers do you have now, sweetie?"

She thought for a second, looked at her iPhone 67 for the four-hundredth time that day, and said, "56.7 million, thank you very much."

"Wow, the world sure loves to follow billionaires' kids around now, don't they?" her dad said.

"Word, Dad, word," she affirmed, knowing her massive list of followers was solely due to her status as the daughter of one of the world's richest men. This fact bothered her, but not much.

Now approaching thirty years old, she was worth nearly thirty billion US dollars, thanks to the one-billion-dollar trust fund established in her name at birth. Another billion year on year, not too bad. Her father, Harold Prescott Ness—indeed, one of the world's new elites—had invented a new social media platform that turned him from a poor coder geek into one of the world's richest men, many years before.

His wealth made him think highly of himself, though—frustratingly to him—few others did. Simply put, Mr. Ness was a rich man but also a hated one. Everyone saw him as yet another twisted, selfish, utterly boorish Caucasian male. He intentionally walked with a contrived, ungainly strut, believing it would yield respect, but it only deepened people's hatred, including his two children. Now on his fourth wife, he had made each sign pre-nuptial and non-disclosure agreements before the wedding, ensuring they received far less than their expected half in the inevitable divorce to come. He was mean to his wives, mean to his kids, extremely mean to his competitors, mean to his suppliers, even mean to his personal trainer. He was mean to effectively everyone. His servants hated him. Waiters and waitresses hated him. His personal pilot in his late model *Dassault Falcon 8X* jet hated him. Journalists hated him. His personal masseuse, soft hands and firm touch, hated him more than most, for reasons that will soon become crystal clear. Even his fellow billionaires hated him. He tried to project an image of greatness, but deep within, he was alone. He was shallow. He was lonely. In fact, he was miserable. He even hated dogs, food, and music. He hadn't touched dirt in decades and despised anyone who toiled in the soil, viewing them as filthy losers.

Despite the luck and good fortune that once followed Harry wherever he went, his life felt increasingly empty. He owned everything a person could desire: seven homes, each worth over forty million dollars; a plane and two yachts; vast sums hidden in tax havens like the British Virgin Islands, Luxembourg, and Panama; and had connections with the rich and powerful worldwide.

But still, at its core, life for Harry felt empty. He had no interest in going to space, like those other billionaires, or in conquering "the illness of death," a goal many wealthy Californians had deployed in recent years. He just wanted to be happy, but happiness never seemed to come. He was terrified, as were virtually all of his billionaire buddies—eighty-eight percent of whom were men and the mere twelve percent of billionaires who were women—that they could lose what they had. And he did everything within his power to make sure this would never happen.

Like so many of the BilliBros, he had a virtual army of security and bodyguards. He lived most of the time behind a retractable drawbridge, installed for three million dollars at his favorite home, located in the Hamptons, but who's counting? Like all of his moneyed mates, he hid many assets behind secret shell companies, private trusts, and other arrangements so the tax men could never get their due.

No matter how hard one might look, you won't easily find the name of Harold Prescott Ness in too many registries of beneficial ownership, that's for sure. Although he owned more than 200 companies, not a single one of these had his name on the ownership documents in yet another successful effort to keep his assets away from the prying eyes of the tax man. On the rare occasions he went out, he did so incognito, wearing various hats and disguises, trying to make sure none of those haters out there knew it was him.

He received so many threatening emails and so much online hate that he barely took notice anymore. He knew he was a major cause of the social cleavages bubbling away in his country and that he and his billionaire brood were responsible for the majority of global warming, the resultant climate change, and outrageous inequality—but he didn't give one single shit. In fact, he was proud of it.

Despite his ongoing depression, he still believed in the credo: "He who dies with the most toys wins." And he tastelessly displayed a related sticker on his *Maserati Quattroporte Trofeo,* which made people hate him even more. His most recent ex-wife drove a personalized Hummer with a gold-plated steering wheel and a sticker reading "My Little Baby." What a fine couple they had been. Poor Harry, now already seeking Wife No. 5, was sad, alone, rich, and despised by nearly everyone, especially the Killionaire.

10

Although he did many not-so-nice things, Lawrence Underwood Lawson was one of the few BilliBros who was actually a nice person. Larry, as his friends called him, and LUL, as his detractors liked to label this single human worth more than 140 billion dollars, was genuinely kind and even interested in people he met for the first time, on the rare occasions that he actually did meet someone new.

Larry, raised on a housing estate in the British Midlands, not far from Nottingham, had heard stories of Nottingham Forest, and Robin Hood and his merry men, *ad nauseum* during his youth. These tales were more central to his adult personality than anything else in the area, including the decaying factories, high unemployment, and some of the palest people anywhere on the planet.

But instead of siding with Mr. Hood, little Larry found the taker-from-the-rich-and-giver-to-the-poor nothing more than a sickening, depraved criminal, not a kind and caring redistributor. No, not Larry. He had internally vowed to never allow any newfound Robin Hood, whether the state or some dirty *povo* gang, to steal his upcoming riches. No way. Larry's interests swerved first right and then decidedly leftward and then back again on the political spectrum, and off he went toward the wisdom allegedly hiding somewhere in the vast wilds of Asia, never to return to his ancestral home—nor even the country of his birth.

Decades after his Robin Hood trauma, he busily redesigned the Mumbai skyscraper he had bought from a new BilliBro, with twenty-eight floors for himself and his family alone. He had doled out nine hundred million US dollars on this monstrosity of a dwelling in one of the world's most polluted and crowded cities. He could afford it, and nothing was too good for his four children. Each trust fund kid got their own floor in the building, a sprawling six hundred square meters of excess (in a town where the millions of slum dwellers had barely three-square meters per person), complete with a swimming pool and jacuzzi, ever so equitably ensuring the children understood the principle of equality of treatment. Level playing fields for all, of course. The building had twelve pools in all, ten of which were in *his* multi-floor portion of the building.

Yes, Larry had made his money through deception, but unlike most other BilliBros, he felt guilty about it. He felt remorseful as he scanned the horizon on rare clear days and saw the hundreds of slums across Greater Mumbai. Having visited these slums many times to distribute excess vegetables and rice, he knew the harsh reality of life there—constant suffering endured by millions, with numbers growing by thousands every day as India's wealth increased. This trend wasn't limited to India; globally, the wealth of the 1%, especially the 0.00003%, was rising, but slums were expanding even faster. The UN predicted that up to 30% of humanity would live in slums by 2050.

I guess India never had a successful Robin Hood, he thought. *What a world.*

Despite often feeling shame-faced about his ultra-high-net-worth individual (UHNWI) status, he felt even worse about how he had made his fortune. He had created a soft drink that, within months of its launch in ever-so-thirsty India, usurped all other brands, rapidly becoming the most popular beverage in the world's most populated country. The drink then spread globally, consumed with abandon throughout the Global South and increasingly in the Global North, always in Earth-destroying plastic bottles produced by workers toiling in utterly brutal conditions, and made with dangerously tainted sugar—lots and lots of it.

During his early years, when he first visited India seeking spiritual salvation with the help of a corrupt, lecherous, and gruesomely ugly guru, he had ordered a Campa Cola. His first sip had shocked him with its lack of sweetness compared to the sugary cola brands he knew from his English hometown. At that moment, reinforced by an equally bland sip of Thums Up, a Seven-Up wannabe, his quest for enlightenment went straight out the door. Instead, he became obsessed with quenching the thirst of over a billion Indians. The guru's demand for sexual favors in exchange for "ancient wisdom" sealed the deal.

"My quest was once enlightenment. No longer. My quest now is to quench," he was often heard to say.

Meeting his Indian wife, Preethi, had made any other outcome impossible, and off he went into the land of hazy sunsets, dal makhani, and the world's nastiest swear words uttered more frequently, and with more conviction, than just about anywhere else.

Knowing that one of the most popular cola brands put forty grams of sugar into each dangerous can or bottle, he decided to add more. He first experimented with a hundred grams, which was too sweet even for the sweetest of all sweet tooths. Then he tried forty-five grams, but it tasted too much like the cola he was used to drinking. He had already figured out the secret recipe of some of the most popular flavors, recognizing tamarind pulp as the key ingredient. So, the teenager within him thought he would rather rudely try sixty-nine grams of sugar per serving, and that turned out to be just right. Easy to remember too.

After that, off he went to access the heavy-metal-laced sugar, tamarind, and water needed to make this—the most popular drink in the birthplace of Buddhism but now the global home of Hinduism. He bought the land needed for the factories, the trucks and the ships needed for distribution, and the advertising to make sure everyone knew about this fascinating new elixir. Then he set about making his billions. Cola brands were never very upfront about the tamarind, but he shared the recipe for his famous drink with everyone.

What he had kept secret, however, was that his creepy military crony friends in nearby Myanmar supplied him with over ten thousand kilos of gooey, pure opium every year. He added a tiny portion to every batch, intentionally addicting billions worldwide to opium and toxic sugar simultaneously, making the notorious opioid family in the US seem like amateurs by comparison. Only his most trusted staff knew about this malicious deed, allowing him to get away with it for years. During that time, hundreds of millions worldwide developed Type 2 diabetes and an opiate addiction, despite most never knowingly consuming opium. This confounded the world, and it took the Killionaire's lab to figure out that this was the real reason why so many people had gotten so sick for so long. And the Killionaire's memory was far from forgetful.

It was this, more than anything else, that made Lawson feel the constant pang of guilt. It wasn't just inventing an addictive drink that prematurely killed millions worldwide that made him so wealthy. He made even more billions on his invention of the serum that allowed people to get over their addiction very quickly to this inimitable beverage. That allowed him to cross the threshold, making him a billionaire.

He named it and marketed it as E-Z Quit. Advertisers told the unsuspecting public that their product could break their addiction to the sugar and tamarind mixture. In reality, it was a chemical compound modelled on an advanced form of Ibogaine, designed to make people forget they had ever tasted Quench, let alone lived with the addiction for years.

No matter how hard they tried, people everywhere just couldn't give up their daily bottle of Quench. Whenever they ran out or just didn't want the calories, they universally felt so bad that they could only think about another bottle. So, on and on they drank from Timbuktu to Transylvania and Boston to Buenos Aires. Bodies made perfect by nature imbibed billions upon billions of litres a year of the product that destroyed those very same bodies and the weak minds that these bipedal beings carried around within their cavernous skulls. So, yes, he had gotten rich getting them sick, and then he'd gotten even richer making them well again. Such was the world today. *Caveat emptor* (buyer beware).

11

Though in many respects the world's billionaires occupied a category of humans set far apart from all other classes of humanity, so much so that they related to one another far more than they related to citizens of their own countries, most of whom they despised for what they saw as their lazy, and often dirty, ways. But other than their wealth and power, they shared little else except for their collective impatience and uncontrollable salivation as they annually awaited two dates. Drooling billionaires were spotted the world over in greedy anticipation of the announcements to come.

First, they eagerly awaited the yearly release of the *Forbes* Rich List to see if they had moved up or down the ladder. Moving up caused glee, while moving down meant calling lawyers, threatening lawsuits, and bedroom trouble that only a pump or a double dose of little blue pills could cure. *Bloomberg* released a new Top 500 list, but BilliBro cared most about *Forbes*, especially to see which losers had fallen off the list, as their *schadenfreude* kicked into high gear.

Second, they eagerly awaited the annual Credit Suisse *World Wealth Report*, which included tastefully produced graphics of wealth distribution across the world. Paranoia swept the BilliBro camp after UBS, its former banking rival, acquired Credit Suisse, leaving uncertainty about the report's future. They wagered yearly whether the authors of this monumental publication would finally put a lightning rod on top of the wealth pyramid instead of just the tiny triangle grouping the world's eighty-one million millionaires, which made most BilliBros extremely uncomfortable.

Being with each other was OK. It was never truly great, but it was at least acceptable, albeit barely. But being grouped together with plebian millionaires… those disgusting six-zero heathens, they collectively sighed, "Keep them away from us! My stupid plumber's a millionaire, for fuck's sake," Larry was once heard to mutter. Truthfully, his plumber, mechanic, real estate agent, lawyers, and doctors ("one for every hole and tube," he used to say) *were* all millionaires. Many had entered the seven-digit class, but this brought no joy to the BilliBros; it simply disgusted them. The billionaires *got* what the millionaires never did: millionaires were clueless until they hit the ten-digit mark, and the billionaires wanted as little to do with them as possible.

Despite their grotesque and random quirks, in so many uniquely indiscriminate ways, the BilliBros rarely bragged about their financial holdings. But the millionaires all too often did, and this disgusted the ten-digit crowd. This was not only because drawing undue attention to one's exclusive membership in the big boy club was seen as *gauche*, if not risky; the Eat the Rich mentality was anything but relegated to the annuls of history. Rather, the real reason was simply that no one really cared. Who cared about small-scale apartment investments? Who cared about housing prices going up or nominal tax rates going down? Who cared if they hired a couple of new staff in the previous year or received a five-figure inheritance? This was small-fry stuff. It was totally insignificant to the BilliBros, and they wanted nothing to do with it or those bragging millionaires.

If you were going to brag, at least make it worthy of a brag, you wealth munchkins, they would think.

The world failed to understand that reaching a certain level of wealth often altered the BilliBros' minds. Fewer than 0.1% of them stayed content for long, driven by some seemingly built-in urge to increase their assets year after year. The 99.99% never really understood this, but the BilliBros did. And yet, it was abundantly clear that it was driving them all mad. They fell for younger and younger boyfriends and girlfriends. They pursued extreme sports, often fatally, and despite their wealth defining their identities, they felt that people liked them only for their money, not for their personalities, humor, looks, or (alleged and unproven) sexual prowess. Nope, it was all about the mammon.

Unable to shake the label, on they went, pillaging Earth down to the last morsel. They couldn't stop. But other people started noticing, too, and they didn't like what they saw.

The word "sacrifice" was increasingly heard in the corridors of political power, in both the Global North and South. Declining England and her increasingly unhappy appendages, which, when grouped together, still deludedly used the term "Great Britain" to describe itself, tended to utilize and apply the word "austerity" more than sacrifice, but, in effect, they both meant the same thing: open doors to the billionaires and others seeking to park themselves and their ill-gotten wealth in the country and ever closing options to everyone else. The rapidly (Dis)United Kingdom even recently had a leader with a net worth approaching one billion-plus, ensuring that no one was going to do anything to undercut the wealth of the wealthy. The same thing had happened in Russia, of course, where a short and sad dictator with obvious plastic surgery and a tragic propensity for sexist gestures—that did nothing but worsen his already dubious standing—had stolen everything he could, sitting atop a power structure protected by greed, sycophants, and more billions.

Even that self-proclaimed bastion of democracy, the United States, had just vanquished a billionaire from the White House, even while another arrogant upstart billionaire was trying to schmooze his way into the center of the executive branch. Saudi Arabia had a billionaire in control, Thailand had just welcomed back its former billionaire leader, who knows how many African countries had to endure dictatorial despots in control who had stolen their country's wealth and placed them into the BilliBros group, and others were waiting in the wings.

For those who couldn't be bothered with the life of a politician, they simply spread their cash around, ensuring that their political minion friends would protect them. And with friends like these, they had nothing to fear. Or so they thought.

12

"Did you see the news today, you gorgeous thing?"

The world was in a raging mess. Bushfires were devastating huge parts of Australia, with the smoke traversing the entire planet. Brutal civil wars continued in country after country, and the Palestinians were again being dehumanized by an increasingly genocidal, racist and *apartheid*-driven Israeli government, backed unquestionably by their permanent ally the United States of America. Sudan was imploding. The billionaire President of the United States was bombing just about everywhere. Ukraine continued to fight back against the illegal Russian invasion, a country also headed by a BilliBro, leaving almost a million Russians dead, but an end to the war seemed as distant as ever. Libya was a mess, as was the Congo. North Korea was exploring a new way of delivering nuclear Armageddon, and the stupid British government had long ago formalized its pro-Brexit vote. There was a lot going on in the world, but why would she care? In her mind, she had it all, and none of these messes affected her in any way, shape, or form.

"Sure didn't," replied Harold Ness's current wife. "Why would I waste time on all that so-called real-world crap? It isn't real to me. All those disgusting povos running around screaming about this and that. Worst of all, they smell. They're dirty. They're gross. Thank the good lord that we never have to mix with that human trash heap."

His wife, or should we say, "current property," given his treatment of women, never watched the news. Why should she? She hated the world, hated the people occupying it—whom she called "open-mouth breathers"—and lived a life unlike most. Though she denied the very existence of climate change, even with its visible effects all around her, she planned her life around nature and the seasons, which were changing in odd ways she could not explain. She knew it couldn't possibly be that hoax known as "global warming," that much was certain.

She and Harold travelled with the weather, spending a couple of months in the Caribbean, when hurricanes were unlikely, then a few months in the Mediterranean—St. Tropez, Mykonos, and Ibiza—before heading back to the Hamptons. They would then check on their New Zealand bunker to ensure it was ready for doomsday. They spent only a few weeks a year at their Mead Mountain Estate, leaving Amber alone most of the time, which she immensely enjoyed.

And on and on it went. Sometimes they would stop off for a few weeks in a major city like London, Paris, or Tokyo, always staying in the presidential suite of the local Four Seasons Hotel (or better) and never bringing less than twenty pieces of luggage each, always Armani. They were the worst tippers. With each destination they visited, the list of those who hated them grew, forming an army of tens of thousands whose lives worsened after encountering this revolting couple. But they didn't care. As long as their private jet was in good working order, beluga caviar was available on demand, and chaos hadn't erupted at their next stop, they continued on their merry way without a second thought.

"Why do you want to know if I watched the news today, baby?" she blurted out in between sips of the second bottle of 1955 Penfolds Grange Hermitage that they had opened that night, each costing a mere $12,500.

"Aaahhh, another twenty-five-thousand-dollar evening, darling. How good is it? We made twenty times that amount in the past ten minutes, so who cares? Not me!"

"Well, drink up, honey, because the news I just heard is a bit scary."

It was January 2020, and the newsreader had just mentioned what appeared to be a novel disease starting to circulate around Wuhan in

China. It seemed to be a variation on the common cold, a coronavirus, and what it was doing to people was indeed worrying. People seemed to be dropping like flies, and emergency rooms were being overwhelmed by desperately sick people, many of whom subsequently died. It seemed to be isolated to Wuhan and wasn't found anywhere else. But hearing this got Hated Harry thinking, and thinking he did.

"Fuckin' A, this is awesome; I can see the dough rolling in already."

"Honey, you know I love *dinero*, but isn't that a little vulgar, making money off a disease that might wipe out millions of innocent people? Even to a selfish soul like me, this stinks to high heaven."

"Well, darling, I don't know what's happened to you lately, but unless we pull in what is surely to be billions of the new money—that those idiot politicians who we control will throw at the problem—someone else will grab it, and screw that. And who matters most, my beloved?"

"We do! We do, honey. Of course, we do!"

"You got it! That's my girl! The way I see it, we have a damn good chance to triple our net worth because of this disease. So much so that we might even hit the global top ten. This is going to be a windfall for us, the likes of which we have never seen. I can't wait to see how it pans out!" he breathlessly yelled with glee in his voice and a smirk the world would never forget. "If I can get through to a few presidents and prime ministers from the yacht, I'll demand that all of them push for a vaccine as quickly as possible and then put rules into place that force everyone to get vaccinated. I have to say, I am rather brilliant because this will sell. It will protect the population as a whole and ensure that billions of new cash will be injected into big pharma, of which, as you know, my love, we are a rather central part."

Three years later, it turned out he was right. He'd trebled his wealth in the span of just over one thousand days. Pandemics pay.

Such a smart man, my hubby, she thought.

13

"Yee ha!" Schwanzkopf screamed with the strange mix of a German accent, a dose of Valley Girl vocal fry and a fake Southern drawl, emerging from his personal rocket after it landed safely. Yes, his personal rocket; every billionaire needs one.

Helmut Schwanzkopf, one of Europe's oldest billionaires, stepped onto *terra firma* from his intentionally phallic-shaped rocket, which many believed was the actual design remit. Still as vain as ever at nearly eighty, he adjusted his one-piece bodysuit and looked straight into the waiting cameras from ARD, ZDF, CNN, Fox, BBC, Netflix, Amazon, a whole host of podcasters, YouTubers, influencers, and others. But before any of the reporters could even shout their banal questions about the constant BilliBro battles over who got to space first, who would pay for the first outpost on Mars, and whose ashes would get shot the furthest into space to mingle with those of the late great man behind Star Trek, Gene Roddenberry, Schwanzkopf (sounding oddly very much like Arnold Schwarzenegger) shouted, "Like, literally, that was totally Kosmic with a 'K. None of that 'C' cosmic stuff; this was full-on Kosmic with a 'K'."

The confused journalists didn't have a retort to that little pearl of inane BilliBro nonsense, so they just waited for sentence number two. He didn't disappoint this time, muttering, "Space is, like, waiting for us. It's like there, up there, and like no one lives there, so yeah, I am like planning to change that. I am going to build my next home on the moon, and it will be ready by the time I am ninety. I am, like, totally into it."

Why Helmut spoke like an Alabaman Kim Kardashian with a ruthlessly strong German accent still confounded people across the globe. And how this incredibly egotistical man, whose vanity and shallowness in everything stunned even the most accepting observer, had made his billions from digging big holes in small countries around the world with no regard for environmental damage, confused every onlooker. He went on his merry way, spending with abandon, trying to convince himself of his immortality—and that he alone was worthy of remembrance and an eternal status.

Helmut wasn't as mean as most BilliBros, but he always left a sour aftertaste at events, with attendees often saying to themselves or others, "Just what was that?" Helmut was obsessed with Helmut. He adorned himself with only the most expensive threads. In public, Helmut wore only the finest suits made from the best fabrics and designed by top fashionistas. At home—across his seventeen mansions worldwide—he wore two-thousand-thread-count dressing gowns and organic silk undergarments. To ease his twenty-eight-year-old blonde wife's paranoia, he also wore a solid yet oddly comfortable platinum chastity belt, which generally prevented him from having sex, despite needing quadruple doses of Viagra, with anyone other than his wife, Sofia, who possessed the sole key to this unsightly device. They used to joke with each other and call it a Dick Chainy.

As the journalists dispersed, bored with billionaires in space, Mr. Schwanzkopf briefly found himself alone, scanning for his eight bodyguards and the limo and realizing all of this was meaningless. His wealth, his rocket, his power, his fame, and the countless zeros at the end of every secret bank account he owned all meant nothing. And as he had this unexpected *satori* moment, a burden was lifted from his shoulders and even the depths of his soul, and for the first time since he was fifty-four years old, without the help of any little blue pills, he got the biggest, baddest boner ever, as he yelped, "Sofia, where are you, Sofia?" Chastity belts are not allowed on rockets, apparently.

Helmut was the world's biggest miner. In contrast to many of his BilliBros, he didn't sexually assault women. But for every woman saved from that horrible fate, he happily ravaged the planet twice as much as anyone else, causing more destruction than any other human ever. Ever since he was a young boy in the wilds of former East Germany, he had loved digging holes. In fact, you could see little holes everywhere around the tower block apartment where he grew up on the outskirts of East Berlin. Officials from the SED, the ruling Communist party, investigated, fearing that Western spies or disloyal subjects were planning a revolution right under their noses.

His obsession intensified after the Berlin Wall fell in 1989. He moved to Russia and, with help from a former KGB official, began acquiring discarded state property for himself, despite being a foreigner. He was a self-made oligarch within a few short months. He stashed his ill-gotten gains in secret tax havens spread all across the world, and moved constantly, acquiring more properties wherever he went, although, not before investigating enough to know what lay underneath the surface. It had all paid off. Helmut had finally become the Lithium King, a title he constantly struggled to maintain. He justifiably felt perpetually threatened by other billionaires eager to claim the title or dominate iron ore—or even the massive royalties linked to the extraction of rare earth minerals.

He dug, seemingly endlessly, leaving little mysterious holes like back in East Berlin, yet larger than some small countries, visible even from the rocket he had launched just hours earlier. Instead of feeling regret for his Earth-damaging activities, he looked down at the visible mines and thought, “I did that, it was me, I am richer than everyone else on the planet, except for those three other BilliBros, and screw them, I’ll beat them one day soon. Watch out world, Helmut is coming for you.”

And with that, he snapped a few quick photos of that portion of Earth he had most recently damaged beyond recognition. He scrolled through the photos, selected his favorite one, and promptly posted it onto his *SuperMe* page. It acquired far fewer likes than he expected. Maybe the world was changing after all.

14

William Puhler's great-great-grandparents came to Argentina to escape the brutal poverty of southern Italy. When they arrived, it was one of the richest countries on Earth. However, decades of dictatorship, disappearances, economic mismanagement, and triple-digit inflation had changed that status permanently. Winning World Cups was great, but even those moments of global glory proved insufficient to turn things around. But Puhler didn't mind. He was known to friends and foes alike as El Boludo Maximo. His adoring fans, though far fewer than his advisors claimed, would sometimes yell "BM! BM!" in a wild frenzy of envious adoration, unaware that the BM tag originated from an English speaker who knew the true meaning of those initials.

His opponents, rapidly growing in number, often chanted "BM, BM, BM!" to confuse this sad man. This made BM question whether his support was genuinely huge or merely a few sycophant diehards seeking to grift themselves into the richer realms of his ill-gotten gains.

It wasn't all that different from that gringo guy up north, surrounded by all those red hats and paranoic hatred.

Known throughout the country as the first oligarch, he had naturally supported the Dirty War during the evil military dictatorship from 1976-1983. No memories of Che Guevara, Evita (or Juan) Perón, Diego Maradona, or even Lionel Messi's wealth could ever restore Argentina to its former glory. Asado couldn't do it. Yerba mate, no chance. Tango, nope. Dulce de Leche, not even close. And, most decidedly, the newly elected right-wing president didn't stand a chance; in fact, he would make things far, far worse than ever before. This once great country was shafted. The people now grappled with a perpetually sick political system, unprecedented poverty, and such low levels of hope that it was nearly impossible to find any.

No matter how often the Argentines deployed the trick of cognitive dissonance in their collective spiral of delusion, deep down inside they knew they were doomed. And none more so than William Puhler, who braved the mean streets of Buenos Aires only when truly necessary. Nowadays, he tended to spend his weekends in nearby Punta del Este in Uruguay, boogie-boarding with his best friend Pablo, who lived there now, having given up on the never-ending decline in the land of the Gauchos across the River Plate. The Argentine lived most of the time, however, in his huge and isolated estate in Patagonia, where he would fly in and out in his private plane landing on his private landing strip whenever the urge hit him.

Puhler made his billions in what he liked to call "forestry," a profession also known as clear-cutting ancient virgin forests and destroying them eternally. "The more virgin, the better," he often opined. He didn't care where the forests were, and much like the famous mountain climber's credo of "Because it was there," he very much thought the same. "I chop wherever I stop because it is there," he once said while surveying his latest jungle wipe-out from the safety of his private, luxurious chopper, which flew low over a previously untouched forest.

But those places were not untouched anymore: the Almighty Puhler was on the scene, driving "progress," unfolding "development," displacing indigenous peoples, and growing his wealth by millions per day—while completely ignoring the destruction he wrought. He had made shrewd investments starting from the 1970s, flying on the wings of neoliberal policies that had dominated for over fifty years. He eagerly awaited *Forbes* magazine's annual billionaire list.

Yes, he sometimes feared that cartels or the slum dwellers of the capital might try to take him out or kidnap him or his family. But most of the time, he went on his merry way, taking more and giving less with each passing year. And, with the passage of time, he would climb the billionaire ladder, get a little bit fatter, and engage in increasingly more meaningless chatter. His bank account was full, but his life was empty.

He deceived himself into believing he was a good man by hosting gala events with wealthy friends or sponsoring hospital fundraisers, though the hospital in question often left patients sicker when they left than when they had arrived. His team sometimes spent months planning these events, charging over one hundred thousand dollars per seat, all to supposedly help people earning less than five hundred dollars a year. One side was fine—the other highly vulgar. He would feel momentary pride during these events, where attendees competed to out-dress and out-class each other. But he knew that even if they coughed up all their assets to help the poor, poverty would continue, inequality would worsen, and human suffering would increase. He truly wanted to help but knew there was little he could do. Soon his life would end, leaving little of any lasting meaning behind.

15

"Are you sure you're up for it, my brother?", asked Nathan.

"Ab-so-fucking-lutely, boss. I know you hate it when I call you boss, but man, you're the boss, man, the big boss man."

Horst had been entrusted with one of the most crucial tasks ever given. Success would trigger the largest part of the Killionaire's plan, fundamentally changing the world, now and for centuries to come, and serving as the human catalyst for a more unified world that finally reached its true potential.

Horstelein—Little Horst—had more energy than ten men. He had taken magic mushrooms hundreds of times, with not a bad trip to be found. And with each successive trip on this naturally occurring fungi, Horst gained a deeper understanding of truth, making his life far more meaningful than he could have imagined as a young lad in a small village near Bonn, Germany. Everyone loved Horst, and he loved them back even more—even twice as much. He intuitively trusted everyone he met and would only give up on them after being mistreated by them at least 101 times. Then, and only then, would he turn his attention elsewhere.

Horst was like walking magic. He could make flowers grow from stone, carrots from clay, and pungent marijuana from depleted soils, transforming once-dead land into a vibrant, deep brown, life-giving dirt usable as a veggie patch for decades to come. He could cook masterful meals with just a few ingredients, and no matter what he created, it was always divine. He exercised with immense determination and cared about his health not solely for himself, but for the world that he sought to improve each and every day.

And now, thanks to his extraordinary skills and because he seemed to know everything about everything, Horst had been put in charge of finding the two islands needed to make Pacifica a reality. He had travelled almost as far and wide across the world as Nathan, traversing every continent except for Antarctica. When asked why he had never gone to Antarctica, he simply replied, "Some places on Earth should never be visited by humans and I, therefore, will never set foot on the icy South Pole." He was savvy, and he was as cool as he was shrewd. Sometimes he was over-enthusiastic and often took advice from hallucinations rather than doctors and healers, but he was a Renaissance Man, and his boss knew this more than any other. If given the task, Horst would do it extremely well. All he needed was an assignment; he would handle the rest himself.

He scoured his memory banks and then every map of the world he could get his hands on. Over and over again, he dissected digital world maps online, zooming in to the smallest details, meticulously checking everything before making a selection, and conducting the initial reconnaissance to confirm if the islands matched their distant appearance.

Only eleven thousand of the more than one million islands across the world were populated, and there had to be a reason for this, Horst thought. He had visited hundreds of islands throughout his life, always impressed by how islanders differed from the mainlanders who controlled almost everything, including….most of the world's islands. Though the islands were perfect in many ways, much of the world was stacked against them. In the modern age, islanders knew everything the rest of the world did, and islander kids wanted products just like kids in LA, Shanghai, or Cape Town. The main problem was that, with few exceptions, the costs associated with *getting* these things, this stuff, to many islands made them unaffordable for the average person.

Yes, most populated islands could support themselves, and many remained outside of the cash economy living in an untainted way at subsistence, but self-reliant, levels. But others wanted to be just like the rest of the world, even if it meant extremely high levels of debt, unsustainable extraction of their limited resources, and a willingness to accept the powerful nations' wishes to control them.

Little Nauru, now one of the smallest countries on Earth, had once been one of the wealthiest due to its phosphate deposits. But not anymore. Now its main source of income came from successive Australian governments, which paid Nauru to hold asylum seekers in detention to keep them from accessing Australia's shores.

Haiti, just half of one island, but an island nation, nonetheless, had once been one of the most prosperous places on the planet. But not anymore. It had degenerated—again—into a failed state, with violent gangs sending terror across the land.

Cuba, still attached to its revolutionary dreams, showed that the people wanted a better version of what those in power offered. The Chagos Islands were now a US military base in the Indian Ocean, its original inhabitants ethnically cleansed and living in squalor in Mauritius, despite recent court victories ordering the British authorities that retained control over the archipelago to enable the islanders to return. Hawaii was still beautiful but facing its own fair share of problems, and huge island nations like Indonesia and the Philippines kept wealth concentrated in the capital cities, leaving distant islands mired in poverty and all-too-frequent destitution. The list of such cases was long. Yes, many islands had benefited from wealthy tourists—Seychelles, Maldives, Ibiza, Fiji, Tahiti—but without external funds, these places, too, would shrivel up and barely squeak by.

On top of all that, nowhere was more threatened by the ever-worsening climate change crisis than islands, especially the low-lying atoll nations of the Pacific. These relatively new nation-states, some not more than two meters above sea level, now faced existential threats due to absolutely no fault of their own. Just as during the colonial period, when islands were "discovered" by genocidal figures like Columbus, Vasco da Gama, Cook, and Magellan, today's islands were at the forefront of the fight against climate change, *justifiably* clamouring for climate justice, restitution, compensation and reparations, funds for losses and damages, and tools to ensure their survival for decades—and hopefully centuries. For those who knew and visited these islands, shared stories with islanders, and understood their unique nature, it was evident that while no one deserves exploitation, islanders deserved it less than all others.

Pacifica would seek to fix this, once and for all. The islands would lead the new revolution of global unity. The new vision of an equal world, a unified world without billionaires, would start and end with the islands. No longer willing to be treated as quaint vassals of the uber-powerful and the uber-rich, islands would stake their claim and bring the rest of the world along with them.

After a month of exploring the entire planet, Horst finally found two satisfactory islands that—at least theoretically—met the detailed checklist his boss had created to guide him. Two side-by-side islands were needed; one bigger, and the smaller one barely visible on the horizon—or preferably not visible at all. Horst's boss had listed the vital criteria in descending order of importance:

1. Limitless fresh water supplies – check
2. Small population or preferably unpopulated – check
3. Difficult, but not impossible to access – check
4. Soil capable of supporting a population of at least ten thousand people – check
5. Located within the territory of a sovereign nation-state with whom the big boss man already had excellent personal relations – check
6. Sufficient room to build an airstrip capable of handling Gulfstreams (but not commercial airlines bigger than an ATR-42) – check
7. Sufficient space for a port big enough to handle the ships needed to bring the building materials and tech inputs required for the new nation – check
8. High potential for alternative energy, including wind, solar, geothermal, and mini-hydroelectric – check
9. Mountains high enough to erect 8G telecoms towers to ensure unrestricted communication with the world – check
10. A flat area 111m by 111m on the smaller island for the guesthouse – check

There were hundreds more items on the list, and the vast majority of those were also consistent with the two islands he found. His confidence was high, and his smile, which was ever-present, was bigger and more Cheshire cat-like than ever before when he tracked down his boss and simply said, "Eureka, I have found them."

Horst then collapsed at his boss's feet, like Pheidippides after running the world's first-ever marathon.

"Well done, Horst. I knew you could do it. So, tell me, what did you find?"

Horst got up, his tanned and almost hairless legs supported by his bare feet. Still smiling and shaking with the implications of what he was about to propose, he stood firm and looked his boss straight in the eyes. "Tofua and Kao in Tonga," he said." We can build Pacifica there."

16

Having found the ideal candidate to create the Earthly psychedelic paradise that would one day be named Pacifica, they needed to visit, check it out, and—most importantly—ultimately find a peaceful and loving way to possess and control it. Horst was unsure why Nathan insisted on acquiring two islands when one seemed sufficient, if managed properly.

During the flights to Tonga and the boat ride to Tofua, Horst finally asked why they needed two islands. He realized he would manage transforming these remote, undeveloped islands into something unprecedented, but he feared that setting up one island would be challenging enough, let alone two. Both islands were volcanic in nature, which was scary, but it also had its benefits. Much like the bells in Buddhist monasteries, the constant threat of a molten bath kept everyone focused on the present, with no thoughts of the past or future, just the here and now. The transportation hassles of getting there for the first ten thousand would be hard enough, and that extra trip to Kao was really pushing it. Kao would never have a landing strip. Those who visited would arrive either by a short chopper ride or a very bumpy boat trip.

From the start, when Horst first learned about Kao, his boss became unusually cagey, exuding a paranoia Horst had never before seen in this normally calm and mystical human, whose fervor to save the world was unlike anything he'd ever before experienced.

"Do we really need two islands, boss? This is really going to make things far more complicated than with just one."

His boss replied in a very rarely heard snarky and snippy manner that ruffled a few feathers on the equally calm spirit of the quirky Horst: "Yes, we do. We have to put them somewhere. We'd be crazy to put them onto Pacifica; it could ruin everything if anyone found out."

"Put who somewhere, boss?"

Silence.

Kao, far smaller than Tofua, was a pointy island, a tiny dot of land with an active volcano and huge smouldering crater smack dab in the middle, forming an amazing sight on the horizon, especially as the orange sunset seemed more and more beautiful with each passing day. Most of Kao was mountainous and essentially formed the sides of a massive volcano that could explode at any moment. The only flat area on Kao, located in the southwest corner of this remote part of the ocean, would host the island's first and only major construction project. Although the rich volcanic soil provided ample water and wild fruit and nuts, everything else would need to be imported until they could produce it locally, particularly on Tofua, where the population would be concentrated.

Consistent with Nathan's request, most of both islands' land masses were well above the highest projected sea-level rise over the next two hundred years, with most elevations exceeding one hundred meters. Even if all the ice on Earth melted, they would have thirty meters to spare, more than enough safety for an experiment of this magnitude. If the myth of the drain at the bottom of the ocean turned out to be true, all the better.

Kao was going to be off-limits to all but six of the original residents of Pacifica and the guests who were yet to arrive. The holders of the secret came up with the simple but effective idea that Kao would be designated as a protected area with no access allowed for any humans except for the chosen few. The idea would simply be sold to the residents as an off-limits nature zone; and why not just let nature be nature, for once? All Pacificans would agree that this was something that should be done much more often across the world, and, indeed, it was.

Before Kao could receive guests, they needed to build a helicopter landing pad and a retractable pier for boats. They would also widen the natural coastal cave to meet functional requirements. Afterward, they would install intensive security measures: cameras covering every square meter, movement sensors, and four thick fences around a soundproof, camouflaged compound.

Horst was given instructions about the order of what to do first to get Kao ready, and off he went to accomplish these tasks. Just before he left, his boss turned to him and said, "Horst, come back for a second. Look at these satellite photos of Kao and tell me what you see."

Horst looked at them again, for the millionth time, and simply said, "I see an island, a volcano, and a tiny piece of flat land, which seems to be made of red soil."

"Right," said his boss. "What I need you to do is build the compound as soon as possible and design a roof that perfectly matches the satellite shots." As I mentioned before, please ensure that the building within the compound will precisely measure one hundred eleven meters by one hundred eleven meters."

Before he had time to take a breath, Horst was about to ask for clarification on the size of the mystery structure, but Nathan beat him to the punch. "All one, all the time; that's why I chose one hundred eleven. The roof must cover the entire structure, as well as the four fences that will surround it. It must be indistinguishable from the prying eyes of the satellites to what it looks like today. Use the same soil to color the plain paint to make sure it matches perfectly. Can you do that?"

"Of course, I can, boss. Anything for you, anything for Pacifica."

Nathan also mentioned the need for state-of-the-art cameras, filming equipment, secure internet access, and the ability to broadcast 24/7 inside of the compound to what would soon become the rapidly growing global audience of the most popular show since *The Sopranos*, *Breaking Bad, The Kardashians*, or even *Succession* or *Billions*. Then he said something of great importance. "Horst, you do realize that I love you like a brother, right?"

"Of course, boss, just as I love you."

"But Horstie, I have to ask you to do something now."

"Yes, my brother, anything."

"I need you to swear to me that you will never, ever tell anyone other than those who already know what we are planning and what we will do on Kao. Can you promise me that?"

"You didn't even need to ask, my man, you know that. My lips are sealed now and always; you can count on me."

And with that, they embraced, as they had a thousand times before, merging their souls yet again with the promise of what was to come.

17

Among Horst's many tasks to prepare Tofua for the arrival of the first ten thousand, he focused on ensuring a constant supply of powerful psilocybin. Knowing that these fungi were crucial for the survival of both Pacifica and the planet, he made his first call, once the satellite phones were operational, to that magical and merry melody maker, the inimitable mycologist of all mycologists, the incomparable Flea.

Her not-so-secret admirer had nicknamed her for her propensity to play her electric guitar like the bass-playing wild man from the Red Hot Chili Peppers, though it had nothing to do with her appearance or any prominent gap in her teeth, as there was none. Her hair was perpetually dyed, however, much like that bass banger for the Peppers. Flea's mycological prowess was known the world over. Paul Stamets may have received the lion's share of the limelight for his incredibly deep mycological knowledge, but it was Flea's comprehensive understanding of fungi and how to grow them both indoors and out, that led Horst to call her first.

Horst's task was not only to cultivate psychedelic fungi across Pacifica but also to build the world's first mushroom-based society, economy, and culture. Yes, sacred, magical mushrooms would form the basis for occasional ceremonial evenings throughout the year—not often, but profound enough for these nights to be something that everyone looked forward to for months ahead of time.

Nathan, Amber, and Jason wanted mushrooms to pervade everything. They wanted mushrooms as a key food source.

Mushrooms for medicine. Mushrooms for building materials. Mushrooms for de-toxifying anything that needed to be de-toxified, including tainted minds and bruised brains. Mushrooms as compost expeditors. Mushrooms for clothing. Mushrooms for decorations and art. Mushrooms for music. And mushrooms for magic. It was a big responsibility, but Horst and Flea working together could surely achieve something major.

They never told a soul, but it was this wonderful duo that years before had founded the secretive group known as the Spooriers. Derived from a fusing together of the words "spore" and "warrior," after a few short years the Spooriers numbered in the many tens of thousands. Posing online as a seed company, those in the know would write to Spoorier HQ and ask for one hundred grams of broccoli seeds, and, in return, would receive, by regular mail sent anywhere in the world, trillions of psilocybin spores, which, to the unknowing eyes of a customs officer, might just resemble broccoli seeds (though they, in fact, bore no such resemblance), but which were much more than that. There was no formal organization, no membership, no vows or initiations, and certainly no annual dues required. Rather, anyone could request seeds on the unwritten promise that, within a few weeks after receiving a sacred package, they would frolic with like-minded friends throughout urban and suburban areas worldwide, sprinkling the living fairy dust from their pockets onto the unsuspecting topsoil.

Once autumn arrived, whether in Lima or Lisbon, Toronto or Turin, or anywhere else in the Northern or Southern hemisphere, the unmistakable mushrooms would suddenly poke their heads out of the ground, almost begging locals to pick and consume them. For those who had enjoyed them, these mushrooms seemed like the physical manifestation of destiny, as if they were morsels of wisdom from a distant universe.

Any human lucky enough to have enjoyed a meaningful mushroom experience would always come up with countless questions. "How is it," they almost universally pondered, "that such a small handful of little ole mushrooms can open such extraordinary pathways in our minds? How can it be that in those first six hours under the sway of the fungi, our minds merge back into the fabric of interwoven life where even the most mortal of enemies could see the love in the eyes of the other, in a space in time where concepts such as 'them' or the 'other' or even 'away' were peacefully extinguished, replaced with 'us' and 'we' all with a constant reminder that there is no 'away.' There is only 'here' (and now)."

Flea could identify every sort of mushroom or other fungi blindfolded, and, with her eyes closed, just by feel and smell and maybe even a bit of ambient vibes that certain types of fungi would release, like an invitation to all who dared. She could fearlessly frolic through forests of all types, as if guided by the fungi all around, and find clusters of these magical little critters within minutes; something which no other forager ever seemed to do with as much speed or grace, let alone agility. If she had to pick a newly discovered outgrowth to look underneath to confirm its genus, and it turned out to be one best left un-ingested, she would carefully replant it, root-like fronds and all, with her magical fingers, which resembled tendrils of delight, stemming from arms covered in tattoos dangling at the sides of a body and being that knew no comparison.

Flea herself exuded a sense of magic that was so powerful, so mystical, that she herself had difficulty in realizing just how substantial it was. Many of those around her saw it immediately, but to her, she was simply herself: a self-deprecating, humble, yet extraordinary blue-eyed beauty with an internal joy boundless in nature until she, herself, noticed it, at which point, she instantly retreated behind a protective shell she had mastered as a form of self-preservation from feeling too much.

"Flea—can you hear me? It's Horst."

"Yes, I can hear you loud and clear, Horstie. Well, sort of loud and clear. We had an incredible gig last night, and my ears are still recovering. For some reason, I started jamming during the end of the third song that we always play in our standard set—"Underwater," it's called—and I got caught up in it so deeply that, apparently, I kept going for forty-two minutes, and the rest of the band just went with it, as did the crowd. It was sort of like one of those early extended "Dark Stars" the Grateful Dead used to play at those Filmore shows in the early Seventies, but I wasn't even tripping. Oh well, after the number of times I've seen the Inner Void, no need to trip further, I guess. Anyway, Horst, where are you? What's up?"

"Flea, you won't believe it. I'm on Tofua. Nathan asked me to lead the vanguard and to start building the best society ever—the world's first truly psychedelic society. What an honor, but what a task! Look, we've pretty much explored the entire island, and there are a few places here and there where we've found some *cubensis* growing, but we need more, a lot more, and that's why I'm calling. Can you come and help us out? Can you be our Magical Mycological Mystery Mamma for at least a year or two to get everything up and running?"

"Send me a ticket, and I'm there, Horst. You know you can always count on me. I'm with Pacifica all the way, mate."

Flea was Australian, but no one would hold that against her, even in Pacifica. She was wise beyond her years, and even more quirky than that. Although frowned upon by the authorities, she had a pet wallaby called Trippy, named to rhyme with the Australian icon, Skippy the Kangaroo. Trippy just showed up one day at her semi-rural house, set on an isolated fifty acres with huge house-sized natural boulders dotting the landscape—mounds of protective rock forms that changed shape almost daily, depending on where the sun was high, high above (and how many of her famous mushrooms she had consumed). Trippy, who was very quick to learn, quickly became Flea's best friend and alter-ego of sorts. Flea would put Trippy into her car, nestled comfortably in a blanket, used as much for safety as to hide her from the nosy officers of the law, and drive to any location where she had to be.

Her psilocybin-producing skills made her popular, a growing client base of inner-space explorers whom she reluctantly supplied with the means to jet off into the great and boundless void within. She only needed to visit an address once, make up a name for the place, and say it loudly to Trippy. Once Trippy heard a word a single time, she effortlessly remembered it. Flea would stuff twenty or thirty grams of dried mushrooms into Trippy's pouch, yell "Brown house!" or "Blue house!" and Trippy would hop to the destination. Upon arrival, the happy recipients would take the vacuum-sealed baggie of Flea's exquisite delights, put the money owed back into Trippy's warm and cosy pouch, and off she would hop back to her surrogate momma, ready for the next mission.

Flea was excited beyond measure that she had been invited to Pacifica and knew it would be life-changing in more ways than one. After many attempts with men—and without so much as a gentle rumble of warning—she fell head over heels for another remarkable woman, known simply as Dr. Julia. No one ever got to know Dr. Julia's last name, perhaps for good reason, but despite the mystery, Dr. Julia was, by all measures, an extraordinary human. Trained in the usual metrics of modern Western medicine, she repeatedly saw that it targeted disease at the molecular level but did nothing to address the actual cause of what passed for "illness" these days.

The good doctor tried this method and that, sometimes prescribing exercise, weight loss, meditation, mindfulness, a new organic vegan diet, and other cost-free "medicines" that often did the trick. Most of the time they worked but not always. Some cases required a more proactive approach, forcing her to write prescriptions for antibiotics, antidepressants, and, on rare occasions, opioids. Every time she sat down with her pad to write these medicinal orders, she felt pangs of guilt and failure that more natural methods hadn't sufficed.

Recalling her wonderful experiences with psilocybin one day, she suggested a patient consider a psychedelic healing retreat in Costa Rica or Jamaica, where mushrooms were legal, to explore how these magical fungi might reset their failing health. Once the first patient to have taken that advice returned as a new person, ready for Life 2.0, Dr. Julia knew she was onto something, and before too long she became known for her unique medical skills. Shortly after that, she met Flea at one of her clinics, and the die was cast.

"Hey, Horst, one more thing," Flea added right at the end of the call. "As much as I want to help, and you know how much that is, I have to make my visit conditional on one thing. You don't need to pay me or give me a huge house or any special benefits, but you do need to invite Dr. Julia to Pacifica. If she comes, I will come," she said, slyly and devilishly.

"Like minds, my friend. She's next on my call list."

18

People everywhere were just sick and tired of the same failing political arrangements, even in democracies where the same old and tired political parties switched power with each election. Regardless of the country, every party—left, right, or otherwise—had one thing in common: they always let corporations, and the billionaires who owned them, off the hook.

Everywhere, it seemed, all across the globe, people wanted change and something far, far better, but they struggled to unify these disparate forces into one. Everything conspired against them—nation-states, citizenships, nationalities, residency rights, income differentials, the global economic system, and everything else. They had no obvious place to gather and turn a new vision into reality in a grandiose way. But things were truly changing this time.

Pacifica would provide evidence that better was not just possible but it was irresistible. And it would begin with a dynamic duo of islands that few had ever heard of and virtually no one had ever visited. Then it would spread like the joyful tentacles of a happy mutant octopus, not with eight arms but hundreds, first attracted to other islands to carry out the experiment. Then it would move on to what islanders worldwide derisively called "the mainland," with a smug—but real—sense that islanders knew something mainlanders didn't. They could feel it in their bones. It just had to happen, and it would. It was now just a matter of time.

They didn't see this revolution taking off in Europe, where so many uprisings of sorts had occurred throughout the centuries. Nor did they expect it in China, Russia, or the sure-to-fail next Arab Spring in the Middle East, where one dictator merely replaced another, over and over again.

Rather, in the grotesque age of climate change, rising sea levels, and the unprecedented physical death of nations, it became clear that islanders understood far more than mainlanders. This revolution would start on an island, spread globally, and be led by an island—and its islanders. This, in turn, would soon lead Earthlings to finally grasp the painfully obvious truth: they, too, were islanders in the universe. Humans were alone in an infinite ocean of space, reliant only on themselves for salvation, repair, and evolution into a species deserving of its unique place in the system of life. They needed to move beyond their obscene status as the first and only species to consciously devise the means of their own destruction, responsible for the extinction of millions of others.

Whether by nuclear bombs, melting ice caps, forest decimation, mine digging, air pollution, the arms industry, mercenaries, plastic production, tainted soft drinks, or any number of other planet-destroying tools, the far-too-fallible human race had found a way to wealth for some, which also opened up the very real possibility of decimation for all.

Pacifica was the last hope, and growing numbers of people knew this. First in Iceland, another fine and renowned island. The right side of Hispaniola, the Dominican Republic, came next; and then Bali, Tasmania (home to the world's first Green Party long, long ago), and so many other islands spray-painted graffiti, and often exquisite works of art onto the ends of apartment blocks—all supporting Pacifica. They became visible, far and wide, no longer isolated to islands. Berlin seemed to be covered with them. So did Santa Fe and then Cape Town, followed by Lima and then Toronto, Amsterdam, New Delhi, and beyond. It was everywhere. The people were ready. They wanted something new and were ready to call out for it.

Viva Pacifica Viva! was airbrushed onto walls in Reykjavik, was seen in Santo Domingo, and then Denpasar, Hobart, and beyond. Soon it appeared all over the internet, tattooed on people's shoulders for all to see, and even used to sell new solar cubes that were one thousand times more efficient than the popular silica-based solar panels, which had once been all the rage.

"As they power Pacifica, so will they power the world" advertisements were seen on every mobile device the world over. It was an epoch unlike anything that had preceded it. Throughout history, as people felt increasingly under threat, the norm had been a massive inward turn towards isolation, border strengthening and a shutdown of the human rights system. No longer. People from all corners of the world, and hailing from cultures as diverse as could be, were starting to come to the collective understanding that the crises facing them were the very same as those facing people everywhere else. Any nationalistic strategy simply wouldn't make any difference anymore. People needed and wanted to branch outwards. They now wanted to expand their reach to the rest of humanity. With Pacifica now as viable as it would ever be, it was in that direction that people everywhere turned.

Pacifica was catching on faster than anyone ever imagined. Now, it was *they* who were winning, not the billionaires and their business and government cronies, who increasingly knew their time had come and gone and were now running scared. The Killionaire knew exactly how to put the icing onto the cake.

19

Jasper's chopper landed as close as it could to the front door of the wonderful, minimalist Soma, now deemed the best restaurant in the world by food critics the world over; no disagreement there. For a few hours, however, thanks to his rancid presence, it would be one of the most unpleasant places to be, as Eijkelje made it clear that only he deserved the best food, service, table, and everything else. As he strode noisily into this beautiful and unique eatery, he shouted for all to hear: "Only the best for the best!"

The whole place heard it as was his intention, of course, which unified the random lucky diners in their immediate collective disdain for the man. Everyone now present in the House of King (though the mastermind behind this extraordinary establishment Bobby King would never refer to Soma like this) shared a loathing for this horrible man, who had just infected four dozen women with an incurable HIV mutation, from which no medical cocktail would save them—not yet, at any rate.

On all other nights, dining at Soma was the dream of everyone who was lucky enough to do so, but not this evening. Tonight, no one could eat through the twenty-four courses of exquisitely prepared dishes quickly enough just to get away from that creep over on Table No. 27—the best table in the house, of course. People dining here this evening had waited years to get a seat in this tiny but fabulous place that put dining in Denmark onto the world's culinary map. Eat your heart out France. Cálmate, España. No way, Nippon. Pardon, Peru.

Dining in Denmark had arrived.

Much to the shock of evil creatures like Eijkelje, Denmark had some of the highest tax rates in the world, a fact that struck fear into him but was accepted without question by the happy Danes. They knew exactly what they received in return from a state largely free of corruption, built on the solid foundations of the rule of law, democracy, and peace. The Danes were confident that their roads were smooth, their schools free and excellent, their hospitals immaculate and of the highest quality, and that the few million people fortunate enough to live there cherished their good fortune. Although their immigration policies left something to be desired, most of what Denmark did and stood for was commendable.

Eijkelje, of course, would never live in what he saw as a god-awful place—where people like him faced nearly 60% income tax, meaning he would pay billions a year to a state that redistributed *his* wealth to the clearly undeserving poor, sick, elderly, and unemployed.

Why in the hell should my hard-earned dollars go to pay for those lazy, self-afflicted losers? What right does any government have to take my money from me and give it to those who don't deserve it? he would routinely think. Indeed, these were the despicable thoughts that ole Eijkelje the Infector was now thinking—that undeserving Dutch billionaire who deserved none of his ill-gotten fortunes but who just kept ramming his way through life, one missile after another, one bullet after another, one nuclear device after another, putting just one more zero onto the end of his account balance.

At that moment, the smiling waitress Helga, a classic blond-haired, brilliant Danish beauty who looked a bit like Katrine Fonsmark, approached Eijkelje's table with immense trepidation, fearfully carrying two plates in each hand, her normal self-confidence shattered by the behavior of such a grotesque man. Trembling slightly, she warily positioned these pieces of culinary art in front of this creature of a human and his unsuspecting date and was barely able to tell them what they had just received.

"This is your seventh course: the Baltic seaweed-infused foam perched atop Swedish urchin and Norwegian razor clam. Please enjoy."

Eijkelje hadn't heard a word of it, staring like a stunned deer in the headlights, mouth open, polluting the pleasant air after divulging the breath of an alcoholic, not even trying to be subtle, and simply said, "Hey you, beauty. Want to come on my boat later and fuck on the bow?"

Helga was too shocked to say anything, having never come across anyone as vulgar as this abhorrent rich man, and quickly stumbled away. In turn, not used to being ignored, Jasper then yelled at Helga at the top of his voice, in German presumably to increase the dramatic impact: "Verdamt mal, Mensch, gib mir eine Antwort! Hey, damn you, give me an answer!"

No one felt comfortable anymore, and the place absorbed the pheromones exuding from Eijkelje's disease-ridden body. Instead of enjoying their meal, people began to flee. Master Chef Bobby King was at a loss and stationed himself by the door, personally apologizing to each guest who left early and promising a free meal in a month to make up for the disruption caused by Eijkelje at Table No. 27 making a fool of himself and generating levels of disdain that were just about at the breaking point.

20

Before the official founding date of Pacifica, a contest was held to design the flag for the world's newest political entity, and the designs submitted were literally out of this world. Since flags had been the ridiculous cause of so much of the planet's carnage, many Pacificans didn't want a flag at all.

"We are turning a page in the history of our species, and so we need to jettison the entire notion of these jingoistic symbols of otherness and think of another way of identifying ourselves," said Jason quietly to Nathan one afternoon during another one of their planning retreats.

He proposed a permanently empty flagpole flying an invisible flag, symbolizing everywhere and nowhere all at the same time. Those who cared (their numbers waning daily) could imagine any flag at the top of the pole, secure in the knowledge that their imaginary flag would exist forevermore—but only in their minds.

Some creatively suggested a flag with the words "This is Not a Flag," but this concept didn't get too far. A transparent, non-plastic flag resembling an evil, oil-derived, ubiquitous, planet-destroying product was also considered but rejected as being just too transparent.

In many respects, the most Pacifican proposal envisioned a temporary flag, comprised of hundreds of drones, flying in formation in the shape of Earth, with a smile gradually appearing after a few seconds. The drones remained lit up for just thirty seconds and disappeared without a trace. It was cool at first, but even this unique way of expressing Pacifica's originality didn't pass muster.

Nathan still favored the flag idea, aware of its clear limits and potential for misuse, but they needed *something* the world could quickly relate to that spoke through symbols as powerfully as words. They briefly considered planting a tree instead of a flagpole, but the idea had too many flaws, including the risk of the tree dying shortly thereafter which would have sent all the wrong signals. Jason reluctantly allowed himself to be swayed by his Kosmic Soul Brother (KSB)—which is what they called themselves, exclusively to each other—but only on the condition that after Pacifica was truly up and running, they would slowly downgrade the centrality of the flag and replace this symbol of unity and shared purpose with something else entirely. At any rate, they were merely the founders, and the people themselves would have to vote at some point.

He proposed that instead of a flag, Pacifica would celebrate *Dia Pacifica* four times a year on the solstices and equinoxes. Each *Dia Pacifica* would be a day of magic potions, sacred mushroom ceremonies, organic dining, tree planting, and general fun—reminding everyone of Pacifica's uniqueness and value, while promoting it as something worth freely sharing with humanity. And this is precisely what they did. Respect for all participants would be paramount.

Instead of traditional holidays like Thanksgiving, Ramadan, Holi, Christmas, All Saints' Day, Carnival, or the Super Bowl or World Cup, Pacifica would create its own unique and, frankly, superior celebration. If people thought Burning Man, the Rainbow Gathering or Confest was special, they hadn't seen anything yet.

In the place of those second-level events, Pacificans would celebrate four times a year with a day-long reminder of life's glories, their extraordinary luck to be alive, their self-reflective consciousness, their opposable thumbs, and their large brain-to-body ratio. They would embrace their cosmic good fortune, unity, entwinement and shared DNA with all generations, before and after them. No need for faith. No need for made-up books. No need for gods or priests. No need for churches or temples or mosques. No need for any religion at all. Just a glance to the sky, a touch of a tree, and the sparkle of commonality in the eye of another soul was good enough for them.

Four peak experience days a year, once every quarter, the Pacificans would ceremonially sip a boundary-dissolving elixir that melted egos, merged minds, and satisfied souls, bringing their shared spirit into sharp relief. This ritual would reinforce their belief in Pacifica's success and its necessity for the species' survival.

On such days, the music surged through the air—notes and chords clearly visible to all who looked. The color orange tasted like the Sun, sounded like a bass note, and felt as soft as the cheek of a new Pacifican baby, born into a new world of promise where past mistakes would never be repeated.

There was no need to make an effort at anything; it would just happen. It would babble like a brook. It would flow like a stream of consciousness in which they all swam; the birds would cackle, the monkeys would giggle, and even the non-existent god herself would shine down upon them with yet another reminder: *There is no god, there is no me, there is no you; there is only us, riding atop the wave of life, just entering the barrel now with so much to look forward to*.

And so it was, as Pacifica came into being, and everyone that had anything to do with it knew it would be different this time. They all knew it was *they* who were the vanguard now. They were all in the right place at the right time and all agreed that it was on their shoulders that the survival of humanity itself rested. And not just that. Their sacrifices, their energy, their vision, and their mutual care would drive humanity to a new evolutionary peak. Pacifica would offer the planet a new source of inspiration, a model for doing things right, and unprecedented hope after so many dark and dismal years.

21

Horst's remit was two-fold. First, go to both Tofua and Kao, letting no one in on why he wanted to visit these very, very rarely visited islands. Second, depending on the outcome of task one, return to Nuku'alofa and meet with the king, prime minister, and other power brokers to negotiate a deal.

He received strict instruction to keep the plans tightly under wraps while becoming as friendly as possible with as many people as he could in this beautiful island nation, to see what he could manage. Given that Tonga was very poor by global standards, with a national GDP of only around five hundred million dollars, the founders of Pacifica were confident that an offer of two billion would secure the islands, privacy, and—most importantly—the autonomy they needed to create their psychedelic paradise in the middle of the very deep blue sea. When a complete stranger—kind and bubbly but still a stranger—shows up unannounced and offers you four times your country's annual GDP, even the most nationalistically-inclined government official would listen.

And speaking of blue, nowhere was the water bluer than here, nowhere was the sky bluer than here, and nowhere were more stars visible than here. Nowhere had more blue whales than here. Everything was blue, it seemed. Everything but the emotions of the place, which were as far from blue as BB King's notes were deliciously proximate.

On his first recon trip, Horst flew commercially to Tonga's main island and then found a boat to reach Tofua and Kao. As Nathan, Amber and Jason's sidekick, he knew the importance of first impressions, so he brought his assistant, the decidedly soft-hued Flea along. If any public official hesitated to meet Horst's demands, Flea's crystal-blue eyes and calming singing voice would charm them into compliance. She could have stopped an entire division of amped-up attacking soldiers in their tracks.

A few years later, Amber, not Flea, would sing Pacifica's new anthem in public for the first time—turning not just heads but minds, as well. This anthem was not really intended for Pacifica alone but for the rest of this fresh and evolving world, which this new political entity was aiming to bring into existence. After Nathan called the remaining members of Pink Floyd, they received permission to use *Interstellar Overdrive* as the anthem's music, bookending the lyrics with the start and finish of one of the most profound songs ever recorded, still as fresh and original now, and as stunning to the ears, as it had been in 1967.

Because Amber had given so much money to the cause, and in recognition that without her there would have never been a Pacifica in the first place, they asked her to write the words for the founding song, which she would sing *a cappella* right before the first notes of *Interstellar*. She wrote draft after draft and constantly asked for input. Finally, after four months, she came up with this:

Oh Pacifica
Land of promise, paradise now
Pacifica, integral part of the whole
Pacifica, here and everywhere
Peace forever and justice reigning
Love, lust, and freedom raging
Pacifica, the planet is ours
Nature will guide us
The haters will deride us
Kindness will be our credo
And all will become really neato!

The sentiments were right, even if the words left a bit to be desired. But Nathan and Jason thought it made the point sufficiently enough, even though it caused a degree of uncomfortable cringe in most who listened. She was their main benefactor, after all, so it was a small price to pay. Before too long, no one thought twice, and this odd little ditty quickly became an international anthem replacing all others, including the now-withered *Internationale*, whose time had come and passed. Although the sentiments of that song were sublime, the world it envisaged never came into being.

As Pacifica's influence gained traction, the world embraced *Interstellar Overdrive* too. Despite the song being decades old, the young and old alike discovered it and loved it for the power that it held. It would drift out of people's homes, cars, bars, cafés, and even some politicians' offices. It was everywhere and, the more it was played, the more life changed for the better. Two years after Pacifica's launch, they asked their followers to play this magical song simultaneously at the loudest volume possible. At midnight GMT on August 27, 2034, some 3.2 billion people hit play at once, and for nine minutes and forty-one seconds, the song guided the world in a new direction from which it could never turn back.

Slowly, the best of the world's finest things had begun to take root everywhere, all thanks to the Pacifican ideal. Cities and towns began searching for the elements of the highest possible quality of life. Roads were given over to bike lanes. Trees replaced telephone poles. Homes became increasingly energy self-sufficient. People walked as much as they could to buy and sell organic food—organic everything.

Nowhere lost its sense of uniqueness, but at the same time, everywhere started feeling like a combination of the best bits of Berlin, a smidgin of New York, a hint of Bangkok, an element of Barcelona, and a trait or two of Melbourne. People wanted to live in the cities again. They became nicer, kinder. Billions of people were waking up to realities where simply the realization that one was alive was miracle enough to be joyful all day long.

Beyond the quarterly celebrations of the beauty both within and without, they also decided to have a celebration day as a sort of alternative to Independence Day on August 27 every year. Wanting to outdo all other inaugural days, including the performance of Bob

Marley and the Wailers at the Independence Day celebrations in Zimbabwe in 1980—how often do you get to start something that is truly unique?—they hired three bands to come and play at the festivities. First, Jack Johnson, an island boy himself, would appear, singing his soft songs about things that mattered. He would be followed by the American band Goose, which just kept getting better and better. The Australian band Alarms closed the show with their new song "Leckmeister," which topped the charts and celebrated world citizenship.

What a night it turned out to be, with each act ending their sets with *Viva Pacifica Viva!*

22

People initially didn't ask because they probably didn't want to know. As time passed, however, many began wondering how Pacifica was funded and who was paying for the massive costs of building this new society. Little did they know that Amber, hater of her billionaire daddy and lover of her beautiful beau, had decided long ago that she would spend her entire portion of the estate, some thirty billion USD to build this new way of living.

Early, massive investments in Bitcoin and several lesser-known cryptocurrencies brought in another sixty billion, adding to subscription fees for a total of one hundred billion to create and launch Pacifica. This served as a springboard to influence the rest of the planet, a process that would seem effortless once people saw what was possible in a world without billionaires, dictators, pollution, poverty, and all the rest.

This was some two hundred times more than all of Tonga earned in a year. Even though some believed with conviction that they could succeed without money and feared it would taint the experiment, realism prevailed, and the embrace of *that* green won the day. That other Green would just put everything into motion.

Only a few countries had budgets as large as that, so with such a small population, getting this dream off the ground would be no problem at all. In fact, they could quite easily finance the emergence of new Pacificas all around the world, and that is precisely what they did. As little as the world would know about the endpoint of their still secret plan, they knew even less about the fact that it was Pacifica itself that had launched the latest crypto craze with *EnlightenUs*, a little initiative of theirs that brought in a 50,000% gain within one year. Lord knows what you can do with money when it's spent in the right way. This was going to be fun!

The Pacifica purists began doubting the financial aspects of the new nation, but they eventually became resigned to the fact that it couldn't have happened without money. When broken down into its constituent parts, they recognized that Pacifica owed its existence to countless thinkers, the minds of Nathan and Jason, Amber's influence, the skills of Horst, Flea, and Dr. Julia, and a global *zeitgeist* moving in the right direction.

But all of this would have been insufficient, and Pacifica's impact reduced exponentially, without the billions that turned this beautiful, life-affirming vision into reality.

Unlike other societies, no one in Pacifica desired financial wealth. None of the founders, and presumably few of the followers, even had individual bank accounts. Personal financial gain was irrelevant; they had all transcended the ego-driven status quo and the still prevailing need by so many throughout the world to be rich or at least be seen to be so.

On the one hand, it proved that money spent in the right way with the right intent and motivation could yield extraordinary results that were good for everyone. On the other hand, however, the dream of Pacifica could not be reduced merely to how much access it had to capital resources. It was both. It was always both. No matter how positive the vision is—clean air, human rights, housing for all, democracy, and so much more—there will always be a cost and compromise. Those who took a dispassionate view understood this, but many Pacificans and their supporters were already uneasy with the imperfect origins of what they saw as their perfect dream.

For anyone who cared to look, it was clear that Pacifica had been financed by and large by funds accrued by a billionaire. These funds were supplemented by money from a cryptocurrency that severely harmed the environment and accelerated climate change. Worst of all, the entire plan hinged on a crime that—though widely supported by the global population—was nonetheless a crime.

Nathan and his coterie knew these truths but unified silently. Without the formula of "vision + money + crime = victory," Pacifica would never succeed. Short-term loss, long-term gain, they all agreed, and they felt certain the world would agree too. After all, they were using the weapons of the rich against the very rich they despised, thus cleansing the money and turning it into a force for good. Same with the crypto, or so they could argue in an effort to rationalize things. And even the crime itself—from which they made additional billions, of course—could be justified along the same lines.

"We are simply going to show the world just how utterly awful these creeps are," said Amber, to which all nodded in agreement. "We're not going to kill anyone; we won't physically harm anyone. In fact, as time goes on, all of them will probably look and think far healthier than when they arrive. So, what's the big deal?" Again, all heads nodded in acquiescence.

Horst then chimed in, "You gotta break eggs to make an omelette, no?"

"No pain, no gain," Jason replied.

"When you choose, you lose."

23

On the surface, the lab looked like any other lab. Located in a nondescript industrial estate in Oceanside, the wonders of science worked tirelessly, forming an indispensable link in the chain that would ultimately change the world forever.

"I was hoping we could get it in without necessarily injecting it with a needle. Isn't there another way?"

"Of course," the woman in the rainbow lab coat said. "We can make it into a powder and disperse it through the air in aerosol form. We can put it in food. We can dissolve it into a liquid. Or we can mix it with an oil, gel, or cream and then apply it to the skin, much like the DMSO craze in the early 1980s. And we can inject it or even disguise a vitamin pill and trick them into taking it voluntarily without them even knowing what it is. There are countless ways to have it take effect," said Shannon, her eyes sparkling at the possibilities. "Speaking of DMSO… remember how Leary wanted to mix some Owsley acid with DMSO, disguise it in a water bottle, and smear it all over the White House handrails when Reagan was there? Dose Ronnie and everyone else so they'd finally make the right decisions for once?"

"Sure do. Those were the days! I might just do that one day if I somehow get elected secretary-general of the UN," said the happy-go-lucky, always-laughing, ever-smiling Nathan. "So, how long can you make it last? I need it to keep them out of business for at least a week." To make the plan work, they needed to knock out five people, possibly in different parts of the world, and get them to the same location within a week.

"No problem." Shannon smiled. "Don't worry. That will not be a problem at all. This part will be easy. It's the transport part that seems the more challenging aspect of the plan. I'll make sure that what we develop will work on all body types and all weights. Just to be safe, I'll create sufficient dosages of every version—aerosol, liquid, crystal, and powder. You'll have enough to put hundreds to sleep for a week or more if you want, with no permanent damage and certainly no possibility of unintentional death. And don't forget: this stuff lasts forever, so if you need to use it again one day, you can do so, safe in the knowledge that it will never go bad."

"That sounds perfect. We just need to make sure you get me the drugs at least a week or two before K-day. It's going to be complicated, but we're going to do it. It will happen, and we will be making history in the process. I can guarantee few things in this life, but the one thing I can certainly promise you is this: the world has never seen anything like this before. Your role in this is going to be small, but central, Shannon. We simply can't do it without you."

Shannon thanked Nathan profusely for involving her in the plan, as it gave her, for the first time in a long time, the sense that she was actually doing something to save the world. She was certain she could complete the task with her usual excellence and perfection but feared that the overall plan was too complicated.

Nathan reassured her that every tiny detail of the plan had been thought through thousands of times. The collective effort of several highly evolved minds had conceived of a plan that was without precedent. The vehicles needed were procured, retrofitted, and hidden for the big day. The destination was agreed on and ready to host the new guests. Everything else was coming along just as they had intended.

"You just worry about the drug, and we'll worry about the rest. This is absolutely going to work." Nathan wished, as did the others, that he didn't have to resort to tactics like these, but they felt that they simply had no choice. The single planet—on which all of humanity relied—was dying. Civilization was crumbling. People, desperate and devoid of any creativity, were beginning to elect fascists, even in countries once known as bastions of progressive political thought and action. Poverty now seemed an irreversible, lifelong reality for billions of people. The world had never seen a crisis like this before.

"And we are going to save the world from one seemingly incurable infection for time immemorial. We have the antidote, at long last. This unique disease vector will leave us forever and will never return. Our collective insanity in ever allowing this to emerge in the first place will never be forgotten. Smallpox is vanquished, and soon this disease will be too."

24

She hated calling him "sweetie" but knew she had to do it if she wanted to keep her job.

"Just one second, sweetie, I need to get some more oil," said the talented masseuse. "Ever since you had your back shaved, your skin seems to suck the oil in even more than before. I'm going to have to buy new supplies by the kilo if you keep sucking it in at this rate. And that's a fact…I'll tell ya, sir."

"Oh, Nicole, you are really the best. I don't think I could live without our wonderful two-hour sessions. You make my life so much better than it already is, and, yes, I know, I have the perfect life, but still." He couldn't see her with his head snuggled in the face hole of the massage table, but if he could have peeked, he would have seen her shiny green eyes seethe with anger, her eyebrows raised in disdain, and a subtle shake of her head at yet another obscene pronouncement from one of the world's richest men. *I'm going to kill you, motherfucker*, she thought.

Harry had neglected to recall during this session, or any other, that Nicole was someone's daughter, someone's sister, or perhaps even someone's wife or partner. Similarly, it never crossed his mind that her bank account may have been smaller than his by a factor of billions. His own daughter Amber was also someone's daughter: his. So, too, was she someone's sister and, as of the recent past, someone's girlfriend and life partner. Harry missed the obvious link and opportunity. He returned to treating Nicole with the disrespect and cruelty to which she had sadly become accustomed.

As much as it bothered her, Nicole felt extremely grateful for her job. It paid remarkably well by the normally far-from-generous recipient of her soothing touch. This enabled her—a single mother—to provide adequately for her two kids. But after years of rubbing down the rotund billionaire, who bore a gruesome resemblance to Harvey Weinstein and who behaved just as badly, if not worse, she was starting to think about other options.

In fact, there were moments when she drove her thirty-five-year-old beaten-up Ford Pinto to Harold's mansion that she felt so much anger at this man and everything he stood for that she nearly turned the car around and thought about another trip to the McDonald's drive-thru to eat her sorrows away. If he was ever outside when she arrived in her car, he would look it up and down and, with a whiff of disgust, turn on his heel and head back inside his eighteen-room house. But on she drove to *Winner*, massage after massage, year after year.

With each passing season, Nicole's shivers of nausea grew stronger at the thought of having to knead the dough of his disgusting frame. Once, she even vomited in her mouth as he turned onto his back, his tiny erect penis awaiting its stroke session. She absolutely hated that part of the job, but every time, she had to do it to stay employed. She'd wanked this fat fuck off enough times to know his every move and sensation, so she could get him to come with increasing speed, thereby reducing, at least by a few seconds, this awful part of Harold's massage.

After one such day at the mansion, not unlike any other, Nicole headed home and decided to stop by the nearby organic café. She hoped to relax with a warm drink, chat with some cool and reasonable people, ease her McDonald's guilt with a chai latte, and then continue onward to pick up her kids from school. She rolled into the parking lot of the bohemian Bliss Nodules Café and found a spot not far from the entrance. She breathed a noisy sigh of relief, free from the creepy billionaire, and entered the peaceful café, where sitar music played, patchouli wafted through the air, and customers and staff softly bustled and mingled.

She found a table, sat down by herself, and had a look at the menu in case there was anything new that she might order. There wasn't, so she ordered her usual chai latte from the hippy girl waitress and then surveyed the scene that was mostly young people from the nearby university. She recognized most of them. Though she had only exchanged quick hellos, she felt judged by them for working for the creepy capitalist on the hill, despite their supposed ignorance of that fact. So, when a nice young man came up to her and said hello, she was pleasantly surprised—and said hello right back. And then she added, "Care to join me?"

He sat down and asked her how her day was. Part of her exploitative contract with Harry on the Hill required her to keep her job details confidential, enforced by a non-disclosure agreement with life-destroying consequences for breaches. But today, feeling the need to unload, she was about to share—with a complete stranger—her even more unusual work life, when he suddenly said, "So, I hear you work for that Ness asshole."

She didn't know what to say. Was this a test that Harry had set up to test her loyalty? Was Harry secretly recording this chat to have grounds to sue her and wipe her out financially for life? The question immediately terrified her, but the percentage of her growing disdain for the billionaire had overgrown the portion enabling her ability to swallow hard and just deal with it. So, she said, "I sure do, but how did you know that?"

He smirked. "Oh, come on, Nicole. Everyone knows you have to massage that creep every time he's around, and we feel for you, girl. We are most definitely on your side, sister."

Completely shocked, she looked around and noticed everyone shaking their heads, letting her know that they understood the truth as well. This, in turn, made her smirk, and she settled into her seat, relieved that the secret was finally out after all of these years. The cool guy sitting with her, his long flowing locks shimmering in the afternoon sun, smiled the smile of a Hollywood actor and said, "You're amazing. Shall we take a walk outside? I have a proposal for you."

Having not attracted the attention of a nice man for far too long, she said, "Sure."

Together, they strolled outside and then into the nearby park—no one else around but the birds (and the bees).

25

Deciding who could and who could not move to Pacifica was a difficult issue that more than once caused rancor among the usually chill occupants. With only room for ten thousand people, demand for the miraculous new place quickly exceeded supply. Too much of a good thing loomed. This required urgent attention. The plan they came up with was—as with most of their plans—rather simple but equally profound. They knew that it would never be a matter of who would be willing to pay but rather a combination of both reason and magic, just like the founders themselves. Selection was based on a mix of commitment, proven track records of improving the world, and a simple lottery. The first ten thousand were chosen and invited to join within six months.

Those who weren't selected could remain registered and get help finding a spot in one of the new Pacificas being established just about everywhere. Many of these were forming independent of any connection with the leadership in the original Pacifica now getting established on Tofua. Others, though, would be actively supported by their overflowing coffers. With over one hundred billion dollars to their name, they would have tens of billions of excess funds to finance other Pacificas where funds were short.

Yet as much as they knew that funds would be a necessary evil in their quest for securing the Pacifican dream, there were rumblings in some quarters that the hypocrisy of wishing for a more equal world without billionaires and the undeniable existence of massive accounts held by the Pacificans could end the whole experiment before it really even started. Their vision mirrored that of Fencie's and they shared the view that no individual legal person could possess more than thirty-eight million dollars. Pacifica had already instituted measures along the same lines, but someone somehow had to be the beneficial owner of all those billions under their direct control. Legally, it would be easy enough to convert all funds into the name of Pacifica, but even that didn't sit well with most Pacificans. They were left with little choice other than disposing of the wealth in the most expedient way possible and in a manner that benefitted their vision. They would distribute the funds, and with that, share the love.

To maximize their impact, however, they would need to be strategic in selecting where to allocate funds. Requests poured in from around the world, necessitating twice-weekly strategy meetings to crucially decide how much money each new aspiring Pacifica would be allocated. They had received thousands of requests for funds and guidance—a huge proportion of which were legitimate and driven by a global desire for genuine change, not the false promises of dictators or populists but *true* change grounded in the shared humanity of everyone, everywhere.

One of the first grants was offered to a small group in southern Argentina, possibly due to local awareness of Puhler and his cronies' nasty antics. Requests came from Nigeria, Algeria, Lebanon, Laos, Japan, Russia, and many other locales, mostly rural areas connected to villages aiming to inspire the births of new nearby Pacificas. Though it had started on islands and many islands continued to pursue the Pacifica path, the movement had expanded well beyond actual islands to include "islands of hope" on the mainland portions of countries. There seemed to be no stopping them now. It was working.

The right-wing, autocratic, and fascist politics gaining traction exhausted people, along with the grotesque authoritarianism fuelled by nationalist sentiments that *never* lived up to expectations. People desperately desired a new and effective system—a system that celebrated human beauty, love, kindness, compassion, and psychedelics, rather than the greedy inequality that dominated other political organizations.

Most people in most places were wonderful humans. Despite their large majority, the angry screams of neo-fascism 24/7 on right-wing media outlets—owned by some of the worst people on the planet—often drowned out their voices. These prime candidates for the Killionaire's attention didn't care one iota about Earth. Indifferent to the fact that there would be no planet left before long, they cared only about amassing wealth during their finite, Earth-destroying lifetimes.

Pacifica required new residents to publicly read the "Pacifica Promise," which outlined their pledge to serve humanity as a whole—not any legal fiction referred to as nation-states or countries. It was time to change how the human race identified itself. They vowed not to use obsolete excuses for bad behavior. As new citizens of this virtual country, they were effectively starting from scratch and agreeing to basic citizenship requirements, just like the basics for new immigrants to any country. As a result, they had to assert the following for all who wanted to hear:

The Pacifica Promise

Every generation is called upon to meet certain challenges, but our generation faces possibly the most complex, multi-faceted, and interconnected challenges the world has ever been challenged by at the same time. Our mutual dependency on this one planet and on each other demands a new vision for the human race. Working together as Pacificans, we can rise to these challenges, play our role in the evolutionary unfolding history of humanity, and contribute to creating a better world for ourselves, for each other, and for all of life on earth.

Each and every human being—all nine billion of us—is indispensable and an integral part of a single web of life on planet Earth.

In the twenty-first century, this web of life is in a profound crisis. Many of our lifestyles are contributing to an unsustainable human culture that is causing rapid climate change and species extinction. If current trends continue for decades, or even years, humanity will face unprecedented peril and perhaps our own extinction before the end of the century. This is a future we cannot allow.

Complicating matters further, a number of other dramatic crises are converging, relating to artificial intelligence, nationalism, political polarization, conflict, mental illness, social anxiety, community breakdown, and inequality.

We refuse to accept that the human journey is coming to an end. Instead, we choose to make our own lives shining examples of responsibility, health, and intelligence. Our actions will determine our fate. Together, we can seek to maximize our own unique contributions, so that humanity might rise to these challenges.

In doing so, every one of us can play a role in the unfolding history of humanity, helping to create a better world for ourselves, for each other, and for all life on Earth.

The sum total of our daily efforts can combine to create an enormous impact.

In this spirit, we commit to the following:

Thinking as a Pacifican

The world in which we live is created by the shared minds of all of us. Human decisions multiplied over many centuries have led to the simultaneous crises we all face. The way we think determines the way we make decisions.

I am, first and foremost, a Pacifican—a citizen of the world—and dedicate myself to living in harmony with the entire human family and all other living beings with whom we all share the planet as a whole. Therefore, as a Pacifican, I will:

Rise each day aware of the Earth we all share, commit to protecting and preserving Gaia for all life, and dedicate my finite life to enhancing our possibilities for a prosperous future for all generations to come.

Promote peace over war, health over illness, fairness over inequality, unity over division, and love over hate.

See myself as a citizen of the world, a national of my country, a native of my local region, and a member of my community and family, all at the same time.

Embrace the oneness of all life and live every moment of my life as a world citizen, benefitting all and denigrating none.

Evolving as a Pacifican

Everyone everywhere experiences the evolutionary and developmental processes of life in the womb, infancy, childhood, younger years, adult life, and old age. The more we evolve as individuals, the more humanity as a whole will evolve. In countless ways, we determine the speed, depth, and distance of our own evolutionary journey toward ever-increasing awareness and potential.

Therefore, as a Pacifican, I will:

Take responsibility for my own physical, emotional, mental, and interpersonal well-being.

Cultivate self-awareness and personal development through a regular practice dedicated to achieving ever-higher levels of consciousness.

Relating as a Pacifican

Our relationships—family, community, national, and global—are vital foundations for building the better world we all know is possible. Continually improving and expanding these relationships will greatly increase the understanding and compassion needed to build a better world. Therefore, as a Pacifican, I will:

Continuously strengthen my relationships and expand my ability to show compassion to everyone I meet.

Work to better support my family, my community, my country, and my world in healing, growing, and flourishing.

Living as a Pacifican

The daily decisions we all make greatly influence the shape of the world as we live in it. As Pacificans, we are simultaneously voters, consumers, citizens, and members of the broader community. The lives we collectively lead will influence the lives of others. Therefore, as a Pacifican, I will:

Be a conscious consumer, using less, reducing waste, recycling wherever possible, and becoming gradually more informed about the source of everything I buy.

Think and say every day: Fuck plastic, fuck weapons, fuck the throwaway culture, fuck materialism, fuck consumerism, fuck fossil fuels, fuck concrete, fuck mines, fuck skyscrapers, fuck discrimination, fuck hatred, fuck individualism, fuck all that shit, fuck!

Take positive steps to reduce my contribution to environmental degradation, increase my contribution to environmental rehabilitation, and live in a sustainable and life-affirming manner.

Take positive steps to reduce my support of systems and institutions that cause harm to human and non-human life and increase my support of systems and institutions that facilitate the flourishing of human and non-human life.

Stay informed about the health of the local, national, and global ecologies.

Monitor my own ecological footprint, including my carbon footprint.

Strive for a net-positive ecological footprint for myself, my local community, my nation, and the world.

Respect, protect, and fulfil all internationally recognized human rights.

Promote the idea of global voting for a global parliament.

The time has come for a new mindset based on the commonalities shared by all people.

The time has come for a new vision of the good life, emphasizing evolution and contribution.

The time has come for a new culture that recognizes the interconnectedness of all life on planet Earth and operates in harmony with it.

The time has come for *Pacifica.*

Viva Pacifica Viva!

Reading and committing to the "Promise" was effectively an informal way of formally inducting new citizens into this new nation —that wasn't a nation. Anyone else could become a digital Pacifican by reciting the "Promise" online. These hastily developed methodologies of seeking some degree of officialdom to their evolving dream had the beneficial spin-off effect of kickstarting new debate and discussion on the broader issue of world citizenship and how to transform this ancient concept—at long last—into a living and breathing reality in which everyone, everywhere was an integral part.

They wanted membership in this new way of being to be *easy* and entirely without any form of pressure or coercion. Clearly, it was an idea whose time had come. The world may have been silently waiting for this for centuries, if not, millennia, with pressure building and building until the breaking point came. Pacifica popped the bubble, and with this release, change was unleashed like never before. Within a single year of establishment, they reached the one billion mark. People from all corners of the globe saw Pacifica as the unifying force for humanity's evolution, the planet's salvation, and, in the eyes of the Killionaire, it was the best way to end the billionaire's evil influence once and for all.

Pacifica worked. It was a way out, a concrete and tangible political formation, which, in actual fact, was not political at all. There were no politicians as such. Nation-states remained in place, but as Pacifica grew, an informal approach sprang into place—an optimistic, fair, and kind alternative emerged, contrasting with the carnage left by nation-states, corporations and, of course, billionaires.

26

Only after succumbing to his initial charm and obscene wealth did the other unfortunate women who had been wooed by Eijkelje gain the courage to share their horrendous experiences with this creepy, evil man. It was awful for all of them. Having endured the most humiliating sex of their lives, they now faced the very real threat of a new form of an incurable disease from this intentional infector, which would ultimately kill them.

For those who spent a boozy afternoon on *Ream Machine*, it was bad enough; but for those who were so unwise as to traverse the entire Pacific Ocean from LA all the way to Bali, it was pure hell. Not infrequently, Eijkelje wished he'd actually gone as far as naming his disgusting vessel *Cream Machine*.

Flea was one of those who had said yes to his propositions years ago in Marina del Rey. She counted every second from the moment they left the safety of the harbor until they finally reached land in Bali many weeks later. He had sold her on a free trip across the shining sea, and she'd signed a non-disclosure agreement, along with a non-compete agreement, promising not to sue before heading off into the sunset. As a result, she was effectively Eijkelje's chattel until they reached the sovereign waters of Indonesia, at which point she jumped ship as soon as possible, settling down in a small village to write her story about those horrid weeks.

She recounted the repeated involuntary sexual encounters, and being threatened by Eijkelje with walking the plank in the middle of the world's largest ocean—where she was sure to meet a slow, terrifying, and horrible death if she went off the end. She submitted, enduring nightly penetration from the owner of the huge, evil floating fortress. Though she occasionally felt a tinge of pleasure, she mostly felt like a victim of abuse, powerless to stop it. And this was, of course, before she knew of the viral load that he repeatedly dumped into her.

On a trip she had initially thought would be so wonderful, there was only one moment that was actually breath-taking in any meaningful way. Early one morning, as the sun rose, she looked across the dreaded bow of the ship and saw two extraordinarily beautiful islands just beyond the handholds Eijkelje used to enter her. Both were pointy in the extreme, clearly made by a mid-ocean volcano, and models of island-ish perfection. Staring at these places and marvelling at everything about them, she wondered if anyone lived there and if the volcanos were still active. Just then, Iene, Eijkelje's assistant, who knew everything but said nothing, strolled by, and Flea asked, "Have you seen those islands off the bow? They are amazingly beautiful."

"I sure have, Flea. I love going past Tofua and Kao on our way to Asia. We use them as beacon points on our route when we do crossings. It's a shame they'll never be the same once those dirty hippies take them over."

"Dirty hippies?" Flea said.

27

Unlike most of the BilliBros of this world, Larry's main assistant was a man. Cedric's dedication to his big boss was legendary. While he wouldn't literally bend over backward for LUL, he would do just about anything else. He coordinated what they vulgarly called Team LUL, which was comprised of planners, media people, investment advisors, lawyers, cooks, personal trainers, and all the rest. And he was on call 24/7. Larry didn't usually call him at hours deemed unreasonable by most mere mortals, but there was one thing that this billionaire simply loved doing, albeit at odd hours of the day. Sometimes the hours were reasonable, but he often chose to enter his exotic flotation tank late at night. He loved to float weightlessly in highly saline water in complete darkness, seeking to let his troubles float away into the endless expanse of space in the only way he knew how.

People generally thought that flotation tanks more or less took care of themselves, but this was very far from the truth. They needed draining, cleaning, and the application of chemicals to prevent black mould and other odd living things from taking root. Trustworthy Cedric handled this task, ensuring that after each of LUL's floating sessions, the tank was ready for the next session with minimal effort.

All too often the phone would ring at 4:15 a.m., with Larry asking Cedric to get the tank ready. Larry nicely provided his handy helper with an apartment in his Mumbai building, so it was just a quick elevator ride to Larry's place. The flotation tank sat on his three-hundred-square-meter balcony, one of over fifteen such outdoor areas in the monstrous dwelling. A combination of fans, outside air purifiers, a plenitude of plants, and constantly spraying water misters kept the area as fresh and clean as was possible in Mumbai.

Most flotation tanks were entirely functional and designed as such. As glorious as the visions to be had were from the inside, they were not all that lovely to behold from the outside. But not Larry's, of course. Larry's pod looked like a giant alien being, replete with color, texture, and a sense of intriguing welcome. There were tiny but highly advanced speakers inside which he always told Cedric to activate precisely three hundred seconds after he entered the otherwise pitch-black and silent chamber. Cedric started his stopwatch the second the door shut. After five minutes, he began playing soothing tunes from the band Oregon on a seemingly never-ending loop of healing music. Even billionaires needed some healing from time to time.

No sound entered from the outside, which was quite a feat in busy and noisy Mumbai. No smells, no light, not even any guru vibes of any sort could pierce through its colorful walls. Inside, Larry was alone, completely, comprehensively, alone. He shut out the world to enter another world—to explore the mystery of his own mind. As he floated more frequently, the sessions grew longer until Larry effortlessly drifted in salt water, Oregon playing, and his mind venturing into realms few could imagine—sometimes for periods exceeding eight hours at a stretch.

And while Larry may have enjoyed these extended trips, Cedric was entirely hamstrung and had to wait within meters of the pod to assist Larry from the enclosed space. When Larry was ready to get out, he would knock three times in quick succession, at which point Cedric would immediately open the door from the outside very slowly and extricate his multi-billionaire boss from its entrails.

I wonder what would happen if I fell asleep or wandered off and failed to answer his knocks? Cedric thought to himself. *I wonder how Larry would respond to that. I wonder if instead of music I could pipe in some sort of aerosol sleeping substance and knock him out for a few free hours of fun?*

Just at that moment, his phone rang. "Hello?" he cautiously asked, not recognizing the number on the screen.

"Hello, is this Cedric?"

"Yes, who's asking?"

"My name is Jason. I'm in Mumbai now and would like to meet to discuss a private business proposal I have for you. Iene, Jasper Eijkelje's assistant, gave me your number."

Without even thinking twice, Cedric said, "Sounds good. India Gate, northwest corner at nine a.m. tomorrow morning, OK?"

"See you then."

28

Nathan, Jason and Amber agreed on pretty much everything of any import. Their views on global history, conquest, colonialism, slavery, occupation, neo-liberalism, and all the rest seemed to merge together like the ingredients in a divine dessert recipe perfectly mixing and matching with an exquisite result to be enjoyed by all. They were rather disgusted by what had so often preceded them. They abhorred these practices, knowing these horrible antics singularly laid the foundations behind all of the world's current crises. They could draw a direct conceptual line to the slums of the modern world and link them to the practices of imperial colonial powers: the slavery and structural discrimination against Black people in the United States, the still-second-class-citizen status of women in so many parts of the world, and, of course, the emergence of the billionaire class and the problems they created and worsened.

When asked by journalists during a rare press conference hosted by Pacifica TV what they hated and what they loved, between the three of them they noted to viewers that they hated fascists, nationalists, autocrats, climate change deniers, racists, fundamentalists of all types and anyone anywhere who truly believed their country or their ethnic group was superior to all others. Conversely, they loved organic farmers, tree huggers, world citizens, human rights advocates, dancers, the socially-inclined, empaths, meditators, psychedelic explorers and pretty much anyone with compassion flowing through their veins.

This trio of evolutionaries had read thousands of books, travelled almost everywhere in the world, and witnessed first-hand the consequences of humanity's actions over recent centuries. They understood the intricate details of how debt kept the developing world in check, perpetually under-performing and beholden to international financial structures and multinational corporations.

These economic dominators exploited their soils, cut down their forests, and polluted their air in exchange for a small bit of coin—just enough to prevent revolution but never enough to elevate these nations to the wealth enjoyed by former colonial powers. Those powers continued to surf on the economic waves of their good fortune, benefiting from centuries of ruthless crimes that now allowed them to live better than any eighteenth-century king could have imagined. They understood fully the power of the US dollar in maintaining US hegemony the world over, and that the eight hundred military bases alone that the US ran across the globe simply wouldn't have been enough without the guaranteed backing of the US Treasury.

And yet…

That such largely boring and uninteresting people could be the beneficiaries of such good luck amazed the Global South. This fact frustrated Pacificans, who couldn't fathom how such materialistic, self-centered, individualistic, fearful, greedy, and awful people—fellow souls, nonetheless—refused to see that having wealth sixty to eighty times higher than similar families in the Global South was shameful. They believed this disparity needed to be addressed immediately to prevent its recurrence.

To the Pacificans, it was self-evident that everyone, everywhere held equal value and importance. All were irreplaceable humans gifted with a single life, whose primary purpose—first and foremost—was to ensure that the next generation would inherit a better, fairer, cleaner, vibrant, and sustainable world. This applied to everyone; everyone except the BilliBros.

With this understanding pervading their actions, the Pacificans grumbled about the impact they might have on Tonga if they acquired access to Tofua and Kao. They discussed it at length to ensure their involvement would benefit Tonga and Tongans and that they would equitably share any financial gains from Pacifica—in a fairer and more just manner than any society before theirs.

They were anxious that nothing they did could be construed as neo-colonialism or domination and developed a plan to ensure maximum respect, maximum equality, and maximum fairness in everything they did. The Pacificans had specific demands and wishes that needed to be met for the plan to work, of course, but everything was transparent and fully shared with the Tongan authorities.

They had the upper hand when it came to finances, of course, with many billions in hand compared to Tonga's GDP, so this would probably seal the deal. Plus, they would do everything within their capacity to be the best possible neighbors. They paid two billion US dollars to the Tongan authorities for the exclusive use of the two islands, based on a ninety-nine-year lease—not ownership—along with a 10% share of all proceeds earned by Pacifica during their stay, a proposal unlikely to be rejected by the Tongan King and government. It would offer a voluntary tax for the right to stay and build a utopia. They would provide jobs to former gang members and criminals deported to Tonga from countries where they had once sought to begin new lives, offering free psychedelic therapies to heal their PTSD and give them a new outlook on life, benefiting the entire Tongan society.

They would exclusively use non-fossil-fuel-powered boats, helicopters, and cars. They would establish environmentally friendly factories, only fish sustainably, farm organically, compost and recycle everything, import and produce no plastic whatsoever, build by using 98% local materials, and generate and exclusively use renewable energy sources. They would commit to fully complying with Tongan cultural mores and statutory law in every way but one—but nothing that creative contract drafters couldn't get around. They insisted on full control over Kao, standing firm in their demands that it must remain a Nature zone—off-limits to all but six of their brood, left to nature alone—or so they said. Tonga happily agreed.

Their secret on Kao was the only deception they consciously chose not to share with their Tongan hosts. Other than that, it was all respect, all brotherhood and sisterhood, good vibes only—only and always.

29

After over fifteen years working in the halls of the UN in New York and Geneva, the World Bank and IMF in Washington, the WTO and ITU in Geneva, and assorted other acronymically labelled gigs in various places across the globe, where the carnage of the neo-liberal vision was evident, Jason Mooi was exhausted. He wanted out. He had spent years trying to get Fencie's ideas taken up by organizations, governments, and NGOs. While his friends gorged themselves, danced the nights away, and scored one true love after another, Jason worked through the night, constantly travelling to the farthest corners of the planet in his relentless quest for a better world.

By now, he had delivered hundreds of speeches in the hallowed halls of the most prestigious economic decision-making chambers, knew the ins and outs of this world better than anyone, and was famous for one particular speech. Just that one in which he had finally felt free enough to pull no punches and truly let loose. It went viral to all corners of the internet, and even somehow snuck through both China's and Russia's infamous firewalls. By now, it had been viewed by almost one billion people. This presentation, which became known online as the *Dish It Speech*, included lines that struck at the core of the matter for Jason and a growing number of people:

> *We all know the figures, we all know the grotesque scale of the inequality that dominates our world, but again, we will fail to do anything structurally to*

address it. Take any of the billionaires in the world today... any of them... and know that if you were to ask them to spend money as an ordinary person would, a person of an average income in a wealthy country of the Global North, they could live without running out of money for quite literally tens of thousands of years! This is absurd. How can we continue to allow this amidst so much war, so much poverty, so much despair, so much illness, so much ecocidal behavior? Let us never forget that the average billionaire creates more than one million times the amount of CO2 emissions as the average human. I'll let that sink in for a moment... Yes, one million times! One million times! This is outrageous and must stop. Who gives them this right? What kind of world have we allowed to emerge, people?

One thing that billionaires know that few others do —but should—is that once someone has a billion dollars, it will keep growing quicker than they could possibly spend it, no matter how hard they may try. And that is why every day, this unjust world belches out yet another billionaire to squash the rights and prospects of the world's poor majority.

After this meeting, just as with the thousands of meetings before, the world's richest and most destructive will again be let off the hook, free to pursue their rapacious ways until there is not one more morsel of profit left to be made.

They will mine the seas. They will cut down every last tree. They will extract every last grain of gold and lithium. They will pump every last bit of oil and gas, and they will frack until they can frack no more.

Tomorrow there will be one more billionaire than there is today, and another added the day after that, and the day after that, and the day after that, unless we once and for all stop this absurd trend. What economic ideology or political thought ever proposed anything like this? Even the queen of selfishness herself, Ayn Rand, would have never accepted this state of affairs. I have read just about everything ever written on economic philosophy and ways of thinking, and I most certainly have never come across a view that says a handful of people should hold more wealth than the poorest eighty percent of humanity.

Which economic theory advocated that billionaires should even exist, let alone increasingly control not just the world economy but the corridors of political power? Who said that billionaires should be able to become heads of state? Not even Adam Smith would have agreed to that! Which book outlined why it was a good thing that billionaires should have no limits on the wealth they could accrue or that these dominant humans would be able to hide trillions upon trillions of their collective wealth in secret bank accounts, hidden in shell companies in tax havens spread across the world? Democracies had aspired to separate the Church and State, but apparently, they weren't ready yet to separate the Economy and State. They were nowhere near that, in fact.

In this very meeting, listening to so many of the delegations here, I heard not the voices of your people, your citizens, but the nagging scream of the billionaires and their cronies who have whispered in your ears, year after year, saying, 'Don't you dare try to take any of our freedoms away, and definitely don't mention taxing us more. You do either of those things, and you won't be around much longer.' That is what I hear when you speak, my diplomat friends. You are beholden to them. They terrify you. Even if they want to kill democracy, you fear them so much, you will do anything to please them. This is not acceptable. This is a disease. If you speak for them, then you too are sick. You, too, are a part of the problem.

At that point, the entire room was silent. All of the usual haggling, wheeling, dealing, and sad attempts by eerie creature-like diplomats to seduce young NGO interns had all come to a stop. All eyes were on Jason, and he knew it. Taking advantage of what was undoubtedly the best speech he had ever given, he then jumped up onto his desk. This had pushed the chairperson to begin banging his gavel as hard as he could, but to no avail. Jason ignored the chair and began shouting the remainder of his historic intervention, no mic needed:

> *But there is a way out. So please, I ask no longer. I beg you all, now I implore you, I beseech you all to please, please, please let us all hear the voices of your people next time. Let us hear the very real clamouring of the call for justice from the billions upon billions of people who are still poor, still struggling, who will never leave their countries, and who will certainly never sit in an airplane or stay in a fancy hotel like all of you did last night. These people will continue to live in the slums; they will continue to flee rising sea levels, losing everything along the way; and they will continue to smile amidst all this carnage—for a smile is all they have.*
>
> *Let me hear the wisdom of those who want more equality, not less, and those who have proposed strong and effective wealth taxes. Let me hear the collective demands, from you, that we need entirely new ways of selecting leaders in the current system that allows the billionaire class to continue to grow without end. Let us consider entirely new methods of expanding global democracy, and let us find a way to let everyone, everywhere, have a say in matters that concern them.*
>
> *Let us establish a Digital People's Assembly so everyone with a smartphone can give their opinions and so we finally ... finally get our politicians to make decisions actually based on the will of the people. Let me hear the sounds of those who believe we are all one human family—one human race, with no one more or*

> *less important than any other. Let me and the world hear these sounds from your many voices. Because if I do, I will know that a new day is coming. One where the world we have built is something we can be proud of instead of something to be utterly ashamed of. Let the new dawn begin.*

The room had stayed silent. If there happened to be a pin dropped anywhere nearby, it most definitely would have been heard. It was so quiet you could have heard their mouths drop one by one—jaws clunking downward. Everyone had been shocked by Jason's universal statement—so truthful, so accurate, so needed by the world. But all of this paled in comparison to what he said next, which truly shocked them. For just when the room and the chairperson himself thought he was done, Jason, still standing on his desk with arms raised, uttered the following line that literally shocked the chamber into a stunned state never before witnessed. He simply shouted with deep conviction: "*Viva Pacifica Viva!*"

After that, the room had remained incredibly still as he got down and politely returned his chair to its original position at the back of the hall. And then off he walked in this quintessential mic-dropping moment, through the corridors of the huge building, going outside through the aging doors, smiling the biggest smile ever. Still alone, the diplomats too shocked to move let alone speak, he strode toward the exit of the massive compound. Then he grabbed his phone from his left pocket, scrolled through the more than five thousand names and numbers, and called Horst.

Horst promptly answered and said, "How'd it go?"

"Horst, it was incredible. I'll tell you all about it soon enough. In the meantime, can you get me onto the next flight to Pacifica?"

30

Jason always seemed to speak first. "There's so many to choose from. How are we ever going to select the lucky winners of our BilliBro lottery? Are we going to be boring and develop some sort of criteria or a selection process, or just use our internal guidance systems, our intuition, perhaps with the assistance of our psilocybin friends or inputs from anyone who might want to suggest an ideal candidate?"

After thinking for just a second or two, Nathan replied, "Yeah, man, let's go with intuition and feeling. If we have to use one criterion, let's select those at the top of the world's asshole meter, and I would like to first propose none other than Earth killer *numero uno,* that Argentine *boludo*, William Puhler—planet destroyer, forest decimator, and overall fuckwit of the highest order."

In 2027, while beginning the planning process for their ultimate caper, there were over three thousand billionaires worldwide. Disgustingly, this tiny group with immense power over billions of people was increasing by one every day, even during the years of the worst pandemic in a century or more. The Pacifican planners thought long and hard about every aspect and believed that if they could somehow get at just 0.1% or 0.2% percent of these democracy decimators, the plan could only succeed, with failure being nowhere near an option or even a possibility. They needed five billionaires, gathered for all the world to see, and once-lucky—now very unlucky —Puhler had definitely made the list.

Unlike that dorky guy who now rode rockets and had huge

warehouses of perpetual exploitation spread across the planet, or that computer guy or electric car oddball, Puhler was not really a household name, but his antics were as deplorable as they were unknown to the public at large. He created deserts faster and on a larger scale and rate than anyone before him, and to those aware of his woeful ways, his propensity for killing hundreds of human rights defenders and ecological warriors who tried to protect the life-giving forests, not just in his Latin American backyard but also in Asia and Africa, made him, well, unforgettable.

Indigenous peoples, whose unceded lands he destroyed for profit, hated him the most, and rightfully so. This single human and his companies had clear-cut or otherwise destroyed millions upon millions of acres of formerly pristine forests, jungles, savannahs, wetlands, and mangroves. Puhler was fine with it, as long as he could milk anything for more cash.

Anywhere, any place, any time was fine with Puhler as long as the money was right. But with each tree felled, each ecosystem pushed into terminal death spirals, and each First Nations people to lose their lands for all time, the Earth became less likely to recover from the destructive forces that had ripped its tendons from their roots, and the human race less likely to regain composure and perhaps survive this worst-ever assault on Mother Nature's riches.

In a certain way, even more heinous than his other crimes were his repeated attempts to deceive the world into believing he was a caring environmentalist, rather than the chief force behind ecocide. He was the master, if not the inventor of, the Great Greenwash.

"Make them think you care," his closest friends and advisors knew him to mutter.

Many environmental-crime monitors who had thus far escaped Puhler and his cronies—who operated with impunity and never faced true justice—were well aware of his role in global deforestation. Fewer knew that his real wealth now came from mining lithium, which he sold at unimaginably high prices to electric car makers who marketed themselves as "carbon net zero" promoters. These companies conveniently ignored that lithium batteries powered the rapidly growing fleets of electric vehicles, thereby fuelling the rise of highly-polluting destructive lithium mines, notorious for their environmental impact, in the few countries where lithium could be mined, including Australia, Argentina, and China.

The average day of Puhler shocked even his fellow BilliBros, let alone ordinary people in ordinary places. Every day—not month, not year, not lifetime—every *day* he emitted not the now infamous one million times the amount of toxic CO^2 gases than the average human. Puhler released twenty times that much; more than 20 million times the amount of CO^2 as the average human! From the moment he awoke until he lay his head back on his pillow twenty hours later—William only slept four hours a night—he was a consumption machine. Nothing could stop him, even though he knew he was a major source of the world's problems and was increasingly despised by those aware of his actions. He frequently walked the thousands of meters of corridors in any given mansion, turning on every light, plugging in every device, running the showers and baths as hot as possible, and activating all the TVs, computers, and stereos—and anything else he could. He would go outside into his twenty-six-car garage at his favorite house in Patagonia and turn on every car at once just to let them sit idly spewing out burned oil remnants, just because he could. He would step back, view the house and cars from a distance, and praise himself as a great, successful man who could say, "Fuck you, humans. Fuck you, Earth." And then his laughter would begin. It would start slowly as a Joker-like giggle, then grow in depth and stature and roll, reaching a crescendo as he luxuriated in his perceived eternal greatness.

A wonderful human.

"Say no more, my Kosmic Soul Brother. Let's add him to the list, for sure," said Jason. "That guy is an absolute criminal of the highest order. Justice must be served. There are no words left to describe how awful he is."

"Here, here!" The others all agreed that getting Puhler onto the list was the right thing to do. Imagining how he would behave when put in such proximity with the other four sent shivers of anticipatory glee through their veins—not for the anguish it would cause but rather for the impact this would have in saving the very species of which all of them were a part.

"Sometimes the end justifies the means, I guess," a woman with a strong Australian accent uttered. Heads turned toward Flea with curious looks, not needing to ask for clarification, which she offered immediately. "We have to get that motherfucker Eijkelje on the list, as well. We need to!"

The others looked at each other, accepting the suggestion but unclear why Flea chose the Dutchman over other choices. They realized that every BilliBro is awful in their own gruesome way. The team turned in unison toward the mushroom *maestra* and watched in horror as tears began streaming down her face. She wept so deeply, so loudly that all they could do was slowly move toward her, offering whatever emotional support they could to the distraught Flea.

Once the tears subsided, Flea returned to her normal jubilant self, much to everyone's relief. No one knew what distant memory caused the sudden attack, so Amber gently asked, "Flea, do you know what is behind all those tears? Can we help in any way?"

Flea knew exactly what it was that caused this uncontrollable wave of anguish to wash over her like a tsunami of pain. And though her mushroom prowess had enabled her to transcend the PTSD most of the time, it occasionally roared back at her like an out of control tiger about to be caged.

"He forced himself on me, the fucker. Repeatedly, the whole way from LA to Bali. I signed on as crew for a free trip and was stuck with that evil creature for weeks, with no escape. He made me hold these grotesque handrails at the ship's bow. He said he would make me walk the plank if I didn't submit, so instead of dying, I endured the most awful weeks of my life. We have to get that fucker. I know you don't want to kill them, but if I'm involved, it will be hard to resist. Life is too good for that scumbag."

Still rather shocked, they agreed to add Jasper to the list, then left the room—energized to get the plan moving as soon as possible.

31

Hunched over a small desk in the bamboo bungalow Horst built during the first days on Pacifica, sipping kava-infused kombucha and sharing a mushroom concoction, Jason and Nathan made the biggest decision of their lives.

"What if we got five of them in one place, like one of those famous St. Tropez parties, and secretly filmed their disgusting antics? It would be like they did in that last Kubrick movie—what's it called again?" asked Jason.

"*Eyes Wide Shut*," Nathan said. "How could you forget?" He laughed and shook his head.

"Remember that scene where they wore masks to hide their identities and create intrigue about the secret lives of the elite? It revealed how revolting and monstrous they were, showing exactly why no normal person would want to emulate them."

"Yeah, sounds good, man, but how in the world are we going to set up something like that? We don't know any of those creeps, thankfully. But even if we did, how would we get them in the same place at the same time and set up cameras to record their mischief? And even if we were able to pull that off, what do you propose? That we collect the footage and put it online? What are you thinking, you wild man? As if they'd care. They'd probably be proud of it."

"I'm thinking about a lot more than that, my law-abiding friend. I'm thinking about something *bad*, something really bad," he said.

"What? You want to kill them or something? You're not a killer, man! And neither am I! Come on, man, be real."

"Well, we might not be killers. But are we truly committed? Are we truly willing to put our ideas into action? Are we willing to stop evil in its tracks? Are we willing to risk our lives and freedom to make a point that could potentially change the world like never before? Are we consequential enough to take that risk? If we won't sacrifice ourselves for Pacifica's vision as a step toward a sustainable Earth, how can we expect anyone else to take that risk?

"We need to do something spectacular, man. Something no one has done before. Something that captures the *zeitgeist*, creates tension and drama, gets those addictive juices flowing, tipping the balance, playing the domino dynamic like a well-tuned lute, releasing notes of change across the world, the entire human race becoming an orchestra of transformation, conducted by the Killionaire."

"What do you mean by Killionaire?" asked Jason. "What a wild word!" I've told you over and over again I am not going to kill anyone, least of all powerful people like the BilliBros. Though I would be the last person to miss any of them, can you imagine the fire and fury that would rain down upon us if we were to take out even one of these rich bastards? They're rapidly killing themselves anyway. Whether in ballooning mishaps, rocket accidents, or submarine tragedies, these guys are dropping like flies. Let the sad sacks die on their own. Let's be creative, man. Let's do something so unexpected, so brazen, so widely known that change would be the only possible consequence."

"OK, so what do you suggest? What should we do then? I'm more than happy to be as creative and radical as hell. We might have a chance then. What do you guys think?"

As they contemplated what to do, the world was falling apart all around them. Climate change worsened at an ever-more-rapid rate. Sea levels rose like never before. Fires were more frequent, widespread, and damaging than the IPCC and others had imagined. Democratically elected governments were undermined by dictatorial forces backed by the ruling classes, seizing power through manipulation. A significant number of Americans supported a corrupt, self-avowed leader, leading to an insurrection, thousands of arrests, and countless prison sentences.

In Guatemala, progressives won an election, but the right wing, in power since the 1954 US-sponsored coup that had deposed Arbenz, resisted. Similarly, Nicaragua, once a symbol of hope, had fallen into one-man rule, reversing the gains made by the party in the 1970s and pushing the country backward. India's long secular traditions seemed to fray by the day. Argentina, not all that long ago one of the richest countries in the world, fell apart at the seams. Tidal waves of new poor desperately eked out an existence. South Africa, despite having perhaps the world's best constitution, never came anywhere near achieving its promise after the end of apartheid, following the rise of the ANC and Mandela. The same happened with Zimbabwe, whose high point was Independence Day, marked by the king of reggae at an extraordinary celebration that never led to the country the rebels claimed to be fighting for.

Russia spiralled downward with each passing year never coming anywhere near its actual potential. North Korea remained as horrendous as ever, while China reverted to a modern-day Mao, with fewer and fewer people interested in what he offered.

There were more wars, more weapons, more deaths than there had been for a very long time. Trees fell, plastic piles grew, and more and more people found it harder and harder to even get by, let alone flourish. Even in the most stable, wealthy democracies, the younger generation found it almost impossible to buy homes, with the job market offering only gigs and short-term jobs, lacking security and pensions. The world was dying, and civilization seemed to be declining even faster. Nice people became mean. Middle-class people became poor. The poor became poorer. The air became dirtier, seemingly hot and smoky almost all of the time.

Drastic times demanded drastic action. Something huge. Something unprecedented. Something that would change the world for the better without hurting anyone, and that would last forever.

32

Schwanzkopf had dug so many holes in so many places that he was tired and wearied, so he shot for the stars instead. Like many other billionaires indifferent to the suffering of billions of humans with whom he shared his life on Earth, he looked up, not to get closer to God but hoping to be seen as a god by all who experienced his unusual ways.

Helmut, still the Lithium King despite Puhler's attempts to displace him, was no different. Ever since watching the first moon landing in 1969 from the discomfort of his East Berlin hot box of an apartment, he remained obsessed with the final frontier. This had nothing to do with the awe-inspiring expanse, the infinite nature of it, the miracle of existence, or the fact that, as far as we know, we are alone in a multiverse of over two trillion galaxies. Rather, it had to do with the simple fact that comets were frequently traversing the sky—some big, some small, some fast, and some slow. What made each of them unique was insignificant compared to what they all shared: their mass was composed of minerals that, if accessed, would make the first to do so the richest person to ever live.

This, and this alone, motivated the young Helmut to transform into the aging space-obsessed Helmut of today. He spent billions on space travel, financed new rocket engines and fuel, and even took a few rides in what he called "the ultimate phallic symbol." He stepped inside the rocket sometimes, prepared for take-off, and mentally transformed the rocket into an erect, somewhat deformed penis, imagining the entire universe as a giant vagina his propelled projectile would soon enter, a sentiment far from unique within the billionaire crowd. This truly troubled and decidedly unwell gentleman—each and every BilliBro seemed to have some sort of asocial aberration—was far from being alone. Despite their differences, these creeps persistently tried to outdo sexual metaphors, likening genitalia entanglement like Moses parted the Red Sea as they distanced themselves ever further from the rest of humanity.

Eddie the engineer was a trusted rocket telemetry expert who worked closely with Helmut. He was now so close with this man of means that he called him "lampshade," remembering a line from a classic Spike Lee film from the 1980s. Helmut charged him with ensuring that everything turned out just right, every milli-second of every flight. But as dedicated and loyal as Eddie was to his boss the rocket man, something began to rub him the wrong way.

His drinking began to increase and start earlier each day—not a good habit for someone entrusted with providing a safe, smooth ride to one of the world's richest, Earth-destroying men. The bartender started noticing, as did the patrons at the watering hole closest to Schwanzkopf's private rocket-launching pad. Before long, word reached the Killionaire that Eddie might be the one selected to turn his *rocket man* into a *boat man* as quickly as possible. This would involve handcuffs, a blindfold, and a strong dose of BGBB (Brain-Go-Bye-Bye), the drug Shannon had developed specifically for this purpose.

After three more weeks of consideration, they did it all over again, with a mastery inconceivable by ordinary mortals. This time, they thought Amber was the best choice. Early one afternoon, when the bar was still mostly empty but the dismal and stale smells of despair had fused into a toxic cloud of unhealthy horror, Amber positioned herself near the entrance. She was visible to all who entered but inconspicuous enough not to draw unwanted attention. As if on cue, at just after two p.m. on what should have been an ordinary weekday, in strolled Eddie, making a beeline to the stained and tattered bar counter.

"The usual then?" asked the barman before Eddie even grabbed a barstool.

"You got it, man," said Eddie. Once accustomed to drowning his sorrows with beer, Eddie now began his daily bout of inebriation with two quick shots of single malt whisky, both downed in quick succession.

Once they had sloshed about in his growing and now protuberant abdomen, he scanned the room to see if today there might—for once—be something of interest in this depressing place. Amber saw him checking her out from the corner of her eye and completely ignored him. Instead, she chose to look down at her phone, pretending to share sweet nothings with an unknown betrothed. She needed to make it seem like Eddie was making the first move so the plans could unfold.

All it took was a single momentary glance, and over Eddie came to flirt to his heart's content. A beauty like Amber wasn't often in his midst.

"Hey, what's your name, big boy?" Amber said.

"The name's Eddie, Miss."

"Call me Amber, please. No *miss* needed. What are you doing in these parts? I don't come here a lot, but I'm pretty sure I would have seen you before, especially given who else comes in here," she said, rather judgmentally.

"I'm a rocket man, Amber. I work over on the launch site for Mr. Schwanzkopf. Do you know who that is?"

"Nope, sure don't. But I guess he's one of those rich guys, eh? Not everyone has a launch pad."

"Well, if a hundred and eighteen billion dollars makes you rich, then he's rich alright. He may be rich, and people think he's a laugh, but let me tell you, Amber—and please don't quote me—the guy is the biggest motherfucker I have ever met. And I've met oh so many motherfuckers. He pays well and all that, but the guy is such a fucking asshole… He treats me like shit to boot. I actually hate him."

"You don't say," said Amber with the straightest face she'd ever had.

33

Plans to get Ness, Eijkelje, Lawson, and Schwanzkopf quickly fell into place. They'd get Ness from the massage table, Eijkleje on his boat, Lawson in his flotation tank, and Schwanzkopf after he inhaled BGBB-laced bong hits just before bedtime. But how would they pull in Puhler? This cagey character moved around so much, often with no warning, that finding the right person to administer the BGBB wasn't going to be nearly as easy.

Flea suggested they travel to Punta del Este, get Puhler's friend Pablo to invite him for dinner, and slip the potion into Pablo's famous garlic and goat's cheese tart. Amber proposed that they get him in Buenos Aires during a fictional lunch with a famous footballer, but that one seemed too risky. And then the third idea popped up, conjured from the brain of Mr. Green.

Nathan asked, "Have any of you heard that Puhler was one of those now-hated BilliBros who bought land on New Zealand's once pristine South Island and built an Armageddon bolt hole there? He planned to flee if things got really bad, not realizing that Kiwis loved the Pacific and would choose the islanders over the BilliBros any day. What if we deceived him into believing in an imminent war, forcing him to flee to his obscene New Zealand bolt hole? He'd only spent three nights there, each night costing twenty-two million, after buying two thousand hectares and building a bunker for a mere sixty-six million. The groundskeeper could ensure the BGBB entered his system by spreading the gel on his golf club grips, or something like that?"

"Hhmm, that might just work, said Amber. "What's the name of that groundskeeper again? She's a Pacifica supporter, right?"

"I think her name is Ra."

"Getting him from New Zealand to Kao would be relatively easy if we used his plane and just flew straight there from Queenstown," his mischievous fellow crime planner opined.

"Doesn't Ra work with us already?"

"You got it, mate!", shouted Flea.

The seller was willing to take sixty-five million, but the buyer insisted on raising the price to 66.6 million just to get his favorite number onto the price tag.

Ra, a Māori activist, had fought for years to achieve greater land rights for the original inhabitants of Aotearoa (New Zealand) and to legally restitute the illegally claimed land, which colonizers stole almost two centuries ago. Thanks to the Treaty of Waitangi of 1840, in stark contrast to the situation across the Tasman Sea in Australia, the Māori had a degree of legal recognition and empowerment that the Aboriginals could only dream about at this stage.

As land rights workers in Aotearoa aren't particularly highly remunerated, Ra quickly took a job as a groundskeeper at a massive new mansion near Queenstown on the South Island. After accepting the job and enjoying the newfound income, it dawned on her that the land where the mansion stood was clearly Māori land, which needed to be returned to its original owners. Once she put two and two together, she would have done just about anything to make that happen.

34

If Nathan and Jason weren't such ardent heterosexuals, they would undoubtedly have been lifelong lovers and married partners. Their connection was addictive at an almost molecular, pheromonal level. They were soul brothers and then some. They shared the same musical tastes, food preferences, and even favorite books. Tom Robbins' *Jitterbug Perfume* sent both of them into spasms of ecstatic joy every time they re-read it, which was generally once every two years. Most importantly, their disdain for the world's economic elite led them to a shared vision of a better world. Each had dedicated their entire working lives, rather selflessly and often pennilessly, to saving the planet. Having concluded that closing the wealth gap lay at the center of any successful approach, they believed that the unnatural, human-made inequality, part and parcel of every society since the Industrial Age, was the key problem to address and rectify—once and for all.

They had traversed the world countless times, seeing time and time, and painful time again, the preventable misery of so many billions of people because of the sickening behavior and power of the world's one percent, especially the 0.00003% percent. They knew that 80% of the world's population barely survived—much less thrived—due to the structural economic obstacles of cutthroat capitalism, and neoliberal theory and practices. To alter this ludicrous stain on the species' reputation, they would make Pacifica matter more than it ever had.

Sharing friendships with—quite literally—people from every

country in the world, they knew at the core of their beings that all people in all places are exactly the same. They knew the oneness of humanity wasn't just some sage bit of wisdom from the days of Lao Tzu or Hafiz, or more recently Ken Wilber or the Dalai Lama, but something that, at its core, was always true and would always remain true. And yet, in this realization, they were not seen as sage dispensers, but rather as dreamers, as esoteric wishful thinkers, and, worst of all, as communists.

Too many people in too many places still didn't get it. They just couldn't break free from the lifelong conditioning that *their people* were the best. That *their people* were exceptional compared to all others. That *their countries* were something worth killing and dying for. That *their people* deserved more than others. Somehow, despite the underlying truth of the commonality of all peoples, this deluded sense of specialness, this ancient art of self-deception, continued to hold sway over the minds of too many fellow humans. Nathan and Jason both knew, in their own ways, that something new had to be done if there was any chance of preserving the species to which they—and everyone else—belonged.

And so this became their two-track dream: eradicate the cause of the disease, i.e., the billionaires, and create a permanent antidote to it ever happening again, i.e., Pacifica.

They concurred about these things for years—while on the road, while in bars, while at concerts, while stoned, while tripping, even while drunk—and kept agreeing and agreeing and agreeing, especially when enjoying the wonderful effects of a shared helping of MDMA. They concluded many years before that if people could see a new vision of society come into being that was so much better than what existed now, combined with efforts to eradicate the virus of billionairism, humanity might just have a chance.

Yet, while they promoted these ideas on their rarely visited website and social media postings, they neither had the business acumen nor the money to make anything substantial happen. But in a way even more crucial than that, they had one major disagreement they simply could not bridge, no matter how hard they tried. Both were pacifists, hence their choice of the name Pacifica; and both were loath to harm anyone in any way, just as they were loath to violate any laws or regulations, except those that involved making naturally growing psychotropic substances illegal. But they also knew that the bad guys out there broke the law daily, flouted every rule and regulation in the book, and lived as if they could and did get away with it. The bad guys polluted without limit, laced soft drinks with tainted sugar and opium, deliberately infected young women with HIV, sold arms to dictators, whom they knew would use them on their own people; and illegally and irreparably chopped down thousand-year-old trees. They happily paid the fine for that final act, given that a single tree brought in hundreds of times the cost of a simple financial penalty.

Why should the Pacificans follow the law when all those evil rich ghouls lived as if there was no law to constrain them? Why should they be kind, compassionate, respectful, and generous when those destroying the world at a record pace lived in ways antithetical to ethical or moral behavior? Why shouldn't these two lovely lads, Nathan the Nectar and Jason the Just, break some rules sometimes, if only to save the planet from destruction? Why shouldn't they become the new Robin Hoods of the twenty-first century, taking from the rich and giving to the poor? Why shouldn't they, with only the purest and most selfless of motivations, bend things in *their* favor for once?

They would often share questions. Why couldn't being a Bodhisattva mean not only delaying one's enlightenment to help others but also dedicating one's life to shifting the collective consciousness away from the mindless obsession with luxury brands, relentless consumption, and the constant pursuit of more, where something people referred to as "retail therapy" was considered normal? People were killing the planet one purchase at a time, one drive at a time, one flight at a time, and often one meal at a time. Something had to give. Something dramatic had to change. The questions then became: what needs doing, when, and by whom? And, more importantly than that, can we do what needs to be done without hurting anyone?

It was in this last consideration that the two beautiful boys had their first and only real dispute after all of these years of mutual—frankly, boringly predictable—agreements. They resigned to breaking laws and taking drastic measures. Every legal avenue had been tried. Every activist strategy undertaken. Every wise word written. Every needed idea articulated. But they had all failed, and the Earth was in a death spiral. They agreed on that, but they diverged on how far to go. Jason favored selective assassination; Nathan drew the line at physical violence. He was only willing to consider kidnapping. Their arguments on this became ever more heated. Clearly, someone else was going to have to break this tie.

Shortly, that person would join them.

35

Iene loved her life on the world's biggest yacht, and as so many who were in the immediate orbit of this or that BilliBro, combined with acts of highest-order cognitive dissonance, transcended the evil deeds of her boss, the HIV-infecting billionaire, Jasper Eijkleje, all in the interest of a huge monthly paycheck. Her massive salary would allow her to retire before forty, with a few million stashed away in a secret account in the Caymans. Jasper, with his many creepy connections in the intentionally opaque world of private banking, had helped her set it up. Loyalty paid.

For the moment, Iene remained as loyal as they come. Despite all she knew about his mistreatment of women, his despicable public behavior, his billions earned by buying and selling killing machines, she stayed quiet and committed to this horrible man. All her obsessive efforts were aimed at preserving her golden cage just long enough to build up the nest egg for a cottage in Bali. There, she planned to spend her days finding soulful beauty and her own form of prana, her cosmic energy, in everything she saw, heard, and touched. It would be wellness incarnate. But reaching those stratospheric levels of radiant health would come only after several targeted mushroom journeys, each time eroding just a tad more of the lingering PTSD all those years on board had brought upon her.

Whenever she had anything more than a few days off in a row, no matter where she was in the world, she headed straight to Denpasar by any route necessary. Upon arriving on the island, she would quickly bypass the horrors of Kuta Beach, overrun by unruly, heavily tattooed Australians reminiscent of a Mad Max scene. Instead, she would head far from the tourist spots, seeking peace and solace in a hidden corner of Bali. Here, among the Balinese who practiced their traditional ways with incredible devotion, kindness, and gentleness, she would find peace. Surrounded by the sweet smell of frangipani, she'd settle in, unwind for a few days, and then share her thoughts on Facebook, believing no one knew her day job—though some did.

One morning, as Iene walked to the local market to stock up on mangos, mangosteens, bananas, and all the ingredients she would need for a fresh batch of gado-gado, for the first time in a long time, she noticed a Westerner also doing the rounds in the frenetic local market stalls. For some reason, this beautiful man stopped her in her tracks. She hadn't thought about sex, love, or attraction for a long time, completely turned off by what she knew and endured as a crew member on *Ream Machine*. In fact, she had begun defining herself as asexual, but on seeing this long-haired god of a man, her juices began flowing like there was no tomorrow.

She went up to him—not the other way around—and simply said, "I've never seen you around here before. Come here often?"

She embarrassingly laughed at her lame attempt at a pick-up line, but even if she thought it not possible, the Shiva-like God before her became even more godlike. He smiled his toothy smile, which melted her to the ground, as the juices flowed ever more vigorously.

"Never been here before," he admitted. He then asked, "How about a coffee?"

She immediately accepted this unexpected invitation. Off they strolled, down the small brick alley, surrounded by smiling fellow humans, fragrant tropical smells, the constant beep of motorbikes and small cars, heading toward the only coffee place for miles—Cafe Kretek.

Something about this man triggered sensations that had lain dormant within Iene for years now. It wasn't just the love juices that were flowing, alas, nearly dripping on the dirt floor of this casual establishment, but much more so, a feeling of genuine trust in a kind and loving Western man. It shook her to the core, in fact, upon the tragic but liberating realization that ever since coming to work for the billionaire, she trusted no one and suspected everyone. And because of the infectious influence of Eijkleje, she had internalized a belief at odds with her nature, that selfishness, greed, and selling killing machines were good—if they got you the world's biggest yacht.

But then suddenly she had a moment of clarity, thinking to herself: *What the hell was I thinking? What am I doing with my life? How could I have been so shallow to work for a man who intentionally infected young women with incurable HIV on his 180-meter boat? What happened to me? Am I really that shallow?* This was guilt by association, pure and simple. Was she really that obsessed with money that she would allow these crimes to be committed day after day without so much as a scoff? Guilt began flowing at light speed through her veins, drying up that other source of watery gush in a nanosecond. Her joy at joining this man at the coffee bar shifted into a deep sense of despair and depression, something Jason noticed immediately as her face, so calm moments before, transformed into a tear-soaked mess.

"What's wrong, my new friend? What's wrong?" he asked as he tried to console the weeping Iene.

Hearing such concern and compassion from a man who just minutes before was a complete stranger, having lived an entire (and very eventful!) life without her even knowing of his existence, just made her cry more. But as she cried, those initial tears of horror at the realization that she had enabled, even facilitated, one of the world's worst men to commit years and years of crimes slowly morphed into cries of relief, tears of tumult becoming tears of transcendence, drops of salty effluvia dripping down her face like morning dew falling down a dusty window as the sun rose in the distance. It created an odd liquid mixture on the floor that defied even the most trusted investigator as to its ultimate source.

As her tears slowly subsided, she found calm and entered a prana space, a realm of oneness with all that ever existed. Realizing that everything had to change, she looked into Jason's sparkling eyes and quietly said, "I think I love you."

Yes, she loved Jason, who was accustomed to being loved by nearly every woman who saw him, just like his comrade Nathan was.

But this love wasn't for his beauty or fortune; it was the kind of love one has for a guru or sage—rooted in trust, truth, and commonality, with nothing to do with gratification or physical desire. It was *Eros* manifesting. *Eros* doing its thing. *Eros* making an unscheduled appearance in Cafe Kretek, merging the minds, the bodies, the souls, and especially the spirits of two humans, two temporary lives suddenly flowing as one down the river of unity toward a shared destiny that just might change the world forever.

36

It took two years of relentless planning, but in the end deep down inside, they knew it would work. They had everything in place: five billionaires enjoying their last day of greedy freedom for a good long while, five secret accessories to the crime, a super yacht for transport, and a brand-new ultra-secret detention facility in far, far off Kao. Only the Killionaire and a few trusted associates knew its whereabouts.

Pacifica was up and running, with the first hundreds of what would become ten thousand souls already building the earthly paradise that would ultimately transform the world. The Killionaire crew knew that Pacifica would only work if billionaires could be banished and drastic measures taken to reduce the gruesome inequality that was now so commonplace throughout the world. But to succeed, no one could know about their plans. Keeping this secret would be no easy task. If they got away with it, the world would be saved. If not, the world would be destroyed. The stakes were high, and the planning reflected this.

Since Pacifica was steeped in symbolism, they knew they needed to choose the most symbolic day to plan their caper. They would need to implement everything about the plan as meticulously as possible—and then some. They couldn't make a single error. They had to consider and adequately plan for every eventuality. They needed to decide the exact minute, hour, and day for these five events to occur simultaneously at five different locations in the same way.

After years of contemplation, the Killionaire had strategically decided on the five targets who would be knocked out by Shannon's unique scientific creation—and would remain that way for at least a week. A year of testing the BGBB had ensured its safety and predictability, wanting nothing more than to keep the five alive and healthy. The Killionaire felt confident it would work.

Transporting four unconscious people to Jasper's gaudy yacht—seeing as Jasper would already be there—wouldn't be easy. But they knew they could do it if they had access to four Gulfstreams. One of them said aloud, in a manner not at all different from what their victims could have easily said, were they conscious: "You can do anything with a Gulfstream."

Oh, if they only knew.

"Use *their* tools against them." And they did.

Could they possibly get all of *Los Cincos* onto the boat at around the same time to make the six-day trip to their new home? Jasper would be an easy target. On his disgusting vessel, where far worse crimes had occurred, they could traverse under the radar toward Kao. His frequent disappearances on cruel jaunts meant no one would notice his absence or that of *Ream Machine*. In fact, everyone felt better the farther away he and his yacht were.

Getting the others to LA unnoticed, though, would be a bit more difficult. Puhler was in New Zealand at his bolt hole, so just a couple of flights away. Ness was in New York, so close by. Larry just happened to be in Tulum, so also really close. That just left Helmut, who was in Thailand doing very bad things to otherwise very good people.

Once the five were on the boat, Nathan would single-handedly pilot the floating vessel all the way to Pacifica, carefully turning off all communication and other equipment before heading off across the world's largest ocean. Then the fake digital avatar of the ship would suddenly appear on the world's shipping tracking websites, and as it would take well over a week for people to figure out that this wasn't the real ship, they would be home-free, all things being equal. Associates had already pulled the ocean-colored tarp across the top of the entire length of the yacht, making it even more difficult to spot from space. They flicked on the water and exhaust disruption neutralizer, shutting off two additional ways to track the boat's location.

Once they had completed the journey, with the engines never turned off, the logistics had to play themselves out perfectly. Upon arrival, the boat would quietly slide into the natural coastal cave, be securely tied up, and remain completely hidden from the outside world, satellites or no satellites.

Once at the secret dock, they would load the five unconscious souls onto stretchers and move them into the compound, one by one. Within an hour of arriving, the task would be done.

They would monitor the chamber via closed circuit TV, ensuring they all woke up at the designated time after dispersing the wake-up elixir through the air filter system. They would watch five billionaires with a collective net worth of over eight hundred billion US dollars slowly awaken from their seven-day slumber, confusedly trying to figure out where they were, what had happened, and why they were in an opulent room with four other humans—all of whom they loathed and detested.

Decades later, when the world found out the details of their plan, there was universal agreement that part of the brilliance of it was using the billionaires against themselves, just as their sensei masters had taught them. They turned their tasteless tools, their money, and especially boats and planes against them. And then, like magic, they gathered the five together in one place in such a manner that when they awoke from their week-long induced coma, they would all be simultaneously in their new digs, sharing a sense of bewilderment and terror all at once, forced by their evil ways to now reside together with their dreaded wealthy competitors, somewhere in the middle of nowhere, ensconced in a structure that was so well built, so well thought out, that they could have been just about anywhere.

Opaque natural light flooded into the structure, but nothing was even decipherable through the cloudy windows. Though much of the roof was glass-like, neither the sun nor clouds—and certainly not the stars—were visible to the five occupants. No one could open the retractable roof unless an emergency took place, requiring helicopter extraction and transfer to another safe location, a scenario the

Killionaire hoped would not arise.

The Pacificans in charge were most proud of how soundproof they had made the structure; neither volcano rumblings, sea sounds, nor bird songs were audible at all. Indeed, there was nothing in the audible realm, olfactory realm, or visual realm that would give *Los Cincos* any idea whatsoever where they were or why. They could be in London or Tokyo, Cape Town or Santiago, Damascus or Hobart. It was impossible to tell. They would feel immediate confusion, then loneliness shortly after that, and within just a matter of days, hopelessness, minute after minute, hour by hour, day by day, month by month, and, yes, year after year.

They wouldn't know where they were, and no one other than the core group of Pacificans would either. In fact, of the ten thousand souls living in what was considered the best place on Earth, 99.99% had no idea that a horrible crime was being committed just one ocean channel and one island away. Tellingly, just as the rest of the world was obsessed with the reality show *Los Cincos*, most Pacificans watched it for a few hours each day, completely unaware that the five billionaires were being held in a prison home so close to their psychedelic paradise. Nothing and no one ever gave the secret away.

Years later, people often wondered what they would have done if they had known. Would any of the more human rights-inclined Pacificans have intervened to release the billionaires? Would there have been an uprising, or would most of the Pacificans, just like the rest of the world, feel a horrible and yet satisfying sense of guilty glee seeing these harmful men, these creeps who had so unjustifiably screwed over the world, finally getting their due? But now, it didn't matter because though a crime was involved, and a serious one at that, the Killionaire crew agreed that no one was to ever be killed, no one was to be tortured, and no one was to be abused. Mushroom consumption, of course, was strongly encouraged but never forced, depending, of course, on one's interpretation of the term "forced."

What *would* happen, however, was some serious financial loss. Not through the usual theft these billionaires deployed against the weak, but through a lengthy series of global political decisions that would end billionairism—once and for all. If the plan succeeded, there would never be another billionaire again. They would disappear in an instant. In what would be seen as a political miracle of sorts, Fencie's ingenious thirty-eight-million-dollar limit would become global policy, and as a result, the world would improve in ways no one could have ever predicted. And, like it or not, many of the changes would result from what happened on Kao. Though few would speak of it, most of the world's population suspected this and, whether correct or not, decades later secretly felt grateful to the Pacificans for doing something pretty bad to achieve something incredibly good.

No one in Pacifica's leadership wanted to do anything of the sort they ended up doing, but after trying for so long to change things through intellectual means, non-violent methods, protests, and all the rest, nothing had changed. In fact, when it came to billionaires and their power, it got far, far worse. Jason himself had written at least one hundred UN resolutions trying to bring about the deep changes needed, but the status quo had remained as firmly in place as ever.

Sometimes people need to break a law to save the law. It had nothing to do with religion or ethnicity, race, color, or even political persuasion. No, this was purely about class, about financial and political power driving the world straight into the ground with nowhere left to turn. They advocated for ending an economic system predicated on never-ending economic growth—an absurd idea within a closed, finite system. They shouted not for the greatness of a country or people but for a new planetary patriotism—for the patriotism of humanity, a patriotism for the people, all of the people, everywhere.

37

In the end, despite all the odds that the plan would be revealed and fall apart, in actual fact it all went swimmingly. Nicole the masseuse, Iene the deckhand, Cedric the assistant, Ra the groundskeeper, and Eddie the Rocket man's rocket man all did a uniquely fabulous and flawless job, and within minutes of each other, precisely according to plan, they had administered the sleeping potion to their special targets, and the race to get them all to Pacifica commenced. They loaded the unconscious BilliBros onto various jets in four diverse corners of the world. Within minutes, all headed to the private and charter terminal at LAX, of course, far from the peeping eyes of the paparazzi and all the rest of LA's media-crazed weirdness.

Nicole applied the drug in the massage oil by adding a healthy dose of DMSO so Harry wouldn't notice a thing. He often fell asleep during his massages, anyway, but usually only after the putrid act this creep forced upon Nicole. But not this time; this time, he had a pre-putrid little rest. Luckily, she remembered to silently slip on a pair of latex gloves right before she applied the elixir, or she would have fallen asleep next to this creature of a man, a thought that again found her vomiting into her own mouth.

Without any real effort, Iene simply spiked Jasper's first martini of the evening and, within seconds of taking his first sip, off he went into la-la land. Just as he drifted off, she stared him straight in the eyes, and —in a last-gasp effort to stay awake—he caught her gaze just as she muttered through her tears, "Fuck you, motherfucker. You're dead."

Eddie's job was a bit more difficult. After infusing Helmut's nightly pre-bed bong hit with a crystallized version of the substance developed by Shannon and the smart folks at Pacifica Labs, Helmut barely had time to say, "Like, wow, this stuff is like totally strong, you know," before he was out cold.

Ra mixed a bit into the batter of the crab omelette Puhler requested for dinner, and he too went bye-bye very quickly.

And, finally, Cedric figured out a way to pipe a gaseous version of the substance straight into the flotation tank. Hearing Larry fall asleep very quickly was music to his ears.

Unbelievable! The first phase of the plan went almost too smoothly. No one was busted. There were no known witnesses. The new drug itself worked miraculously, and all the unconscious rich folks were promptly on their way to the City of Angels. One by one, in quick succession, the Gulfstreams landed and taxied to a distant corner of the airport where they would go largely unnoticed. The crews unloaded each plane with the dozens upon dozens of bags that were always a part of the private plane scene, including, very conveniently, giant over-sized golf bags that fit the best clubs that money could buy, just as easily as they could fit an adult male, even rather rotund ones. They bundled the four into an awaiting white and windowless van and off they drove, completely unchecked by security as they exited the airport, Amber's waving arm and seductive smile ensuring no one would bother to look inside.

Down the LA freeway they went for just a short, ten-minute drive, mostly traffic-free, for once. Upon arriving at the port, they radioed Iene, who was waiting in a secluded part of the harbor. Thanks to a quick moment of passion with the harbor master, all the security cameras had been switched off for an hour. He thought it was just yet another drug deal, but little did he know. That was more than enough time to get them from the van and onto the yacht, which they did with quick and quiet efficiency, knowing that if they succeeded in this caper, they would change the world forever.

Iene had prepared a guest room for the lads and, one by one, the Killionaire placed the sleeping billionaires onto secure, comfortable beds, ready for the six-day journey to Kao—well before the drug would wear off. A final safety check, fuel check, supplies check, a radio call to the harbor master, and off they went. But not without turning off all communications equipment and going black into the night, invisible to everyone—a last hope for humanity. The seas, calm that time of year, made the six-day journey easily achievable, especially with the multi-talented Iene and her Pacifican friends by her side the whole way there.

The days flew by and, after an uneventful journey at full power, and despite fears that the passengers might awake prior to reaching their destination, very early on the morning of the sixth day, just as the glorious sun was rising, they spotted Tofua and Kao for the first time. The excitement and energy were palpable. According to the plan, when they saw Pacifica for the first time on this fateful journey, they would turn on their radio for a second to see if there had been any urgent or emergency messages sent. As there were none, they remained in the clear. They took a wide turn away from Tofua and looped back toward the only access point on Kao. Once they arrived, they launched the thirty-foot Zodiac off the davits, loaded the golf bags, and headed off to the excited Horst and Flea, who welcomed them with open arms.

They quickly bundled the BilliBros into the invisible prison that would be their temporary home, removed the still-unconscious men from the bags, and placed each of them into their extremely luxurious cells. Then they waited for them to awaken, which they did twenty-four hours later, just about simultaneously. As planned, the cameras were turned on as the doors closed—and stayed on for a very long time to come.

38

Over the course of decades, so many movements had risen, and then as quickly as they found themselves on the front pages of the newspapers of the world, rather suddenly faded from sight, perhaps leaving a crumb of impact, but the core of the systems that led to their creation in the first place remained as dominant as they ever were. The post-World War II period witnessed what many thought was an irreversible rise of social democracies in country after country. But in the first years of the 21st Century something entirely different became painfully visible. Rather than social democracy and the attributes of human rights, progressive politics and reduced inequality, the opposite occurred with devastating results.

In response, another series of popular movements rose to tackle these new realities. But did any of them really succeed in a world where inequality had worsened beyond measure, climate change had worsened at a speed and scale never expected, and poverty, disease, war, and disaster had become the norm? Even though it wasn't official policy, in *de facto* terms the world had become a place of walled city-states much like those envisaged in the film *Code 46*. These heavily fortified territories had popped up everywhere. It all started with gated communities and ended up like this; it almost had to. Increasingly, the billionaires would only go to those islands of clean air, serenity, and affluence as they awaited their departure to the rotating spaceship above them to be able to take on new occupants or even maybe settle on Mars, where the first colony was under construction.

If their plan was to work, Pacifica needed to show as graphically as possible just how important it was to end the very existence of billionairism by simply ending the possibility of anyone, anywhere, *ever* amassing such levels of wealth. They had the clear-eyed vision of Fencie to limit the amount of wealth that any individual should be able to have under their possession and control, the famous thirty-eight-million-dollar threshold. They had, themselves, amassed sufficient evidence that the minute-by-minute behavior exhibited by so many billionaires would surely be enough to convince the undecided fence-sitters, many of whom still admired these power holders and deludedly thought of them as forces for good rather than the forces of evil that they all too often turned out to be.

But, all three minds at once thought, *how could they make this more convincing to as many people as possible*? *How can we make it so that not just the politically active portion of the population would come to truly know these BilliBros*? *How can we get an ordinary grandmother, happy-go-lucky second cousin, hardworking farmer, and ardent sports fan to see just how awful this financial elite truly was for them and the world? How could these horrible people once and for all be exposed for who they were and what they stood for? How can we make this happen?* thought the merged mind of the Killionaire as they kept working out strategy and tactics, every day coming just a bit closer to finding the way forward.

Leaking the name "Killionaire" and subtly suggesting that a single individual was behind the crime of the century proved to be a stroke of brilliance. Almost everyone fell for it. Normally, the media or police created names for well-known criminals, but this time, it was the culprits themselves, the minds behind Pacifica. "We only need a certain amount of time. With every bit of confusion we can sow, it will give us extra flexibility. Sooner or later, in all likelihood, someone is going to make the pretty obvious link between us, the end of billionairism, the existence of Pacifica, and *Los Cincos*," said Nathan.

"If we're clever, it might just work," said Amber, feeling every bit as guilty—and excitedly justified—as everyone else.

Much like the credo of hiding in plain sight, Pacifica began broadcasting to anyone who tuned in to the daily reality of the five

BilliBros in captivity as soon as they woke up. Brazen and almost asking for trouble, they aimed to muddy the waters long enough for the plan to work, just as Amber had said.

Backed by monumental global political changes, and Amber's billions, as she remained ever so loyal to Nathan and disloyal to her dear old abusive dad, the plan of plans went into full swing. If everything went smoothly, Pacifica would soon settle into its steady-state population of ten thousand souls, the first to inhabit this pristine psychedelic paradise—before the arrival of the BilliBros. Indeed, that is precisely what occurred.

Neighboring Kao became the stage for what would become the most addictive reality show series ever produced—the first truly global reality show broadcast non-stop. It generated as much gloating and laughter in Beijing as in Boston, Bosnia, Botswana, Belgium and even Buenos Aires, where Mr. William Puhler began his career, a process that would eventually lead to him becoming one of the central cast members of the world's best streaming series ever. And, best yet, it was live, 24/7.

The cameras never stopped. While watching *Los Cincos*, the viewer heard no commentary, no ads, no analysis, just the unsuspecting actors in this involuntary saga revealing everything to a less-than-adoring world. This was the *Truman Show*, *Big Brother*, *Squid Game*, and so many others all rolled into one and then some. But best of all, it was real and the actors had no idea whatsoever they were being constantly filmed. Seven other shows sprang up, each with the sole purpose of analyzing the very public world of *Los Cincos*. But if one watched any of these offerings, one would miss the real show. Choices, choices, choices. When you choose, you lose. As the world learned, when you choose to become a billionaire, you lose, lose, lose, and then lose again.

39

It dawned on Jason that he hadn't been on Pacifica since the very early days, when only the vanguard had arrived and begun their work. The progress Horst and his loyal sidekick Flea had made overwhelmed him, all with the help of very highly paid workers from Tonga who had joyfully sung island songs as they constructed the world's first truly ecological psychedelic paradise.

Replete with a fossil-fuel-free energy grid and regenerative doughnut economy, it worked even better than many of Europe's major cities. A sense of belonging and community emerged that hadn't been felt in the US since the Sixties. So much unrealized potential had been lost to excess consumption, with dismal results. On Pacifica, within seconds, he felt more at home, calmer, and more hopeful than he ever had throughout his entire life.

Yes, he felt guilty about arriving on the Pacifica Gulfstream plane, though not for any climatic problems it might cause. The Pacificans had retrofitted these destructive flying machines, owned by all the BilliBros, with shattering innovations: solar wings, fuselages, and batteries that used fuel supplies made from old cooking oil, transforming a key source of decimation into a cleaner form of transport than trains and electric cars.

Jason's guilt stemmed not from how he got to Pacifica but from the incredible privilege of being there at all. How did he of all people get so lucky to be a core part of this wholly unique human experiment? How was it that he was one of the ten thousand and not—at least for the moment—one of those billions upon billions of his fellow humans who continued to languish in the ever-worsening slums of the world? *If this isn't privilege, I don't know what is*, he thought. Money, fame, or ego had never driven him. Nothing of the sort. It was true empathy, a deep level of compassion and concern for his fellow humans and love for the planet that had fuelled him—and so many others—to push for the changes needed to preserve Earth and secure the basic rights of every human, everywhere.

He made absolutely no distinction between himself and all other humans. A person's nationality did not matter at all. Nor did color, race, religion, ethnicity, class, political opinion, or anything else. No. It was the simple humanity all humans shared—a fact that seemed to have been forgotten by far too many—that drove him from his college years until now. He knew all suffering was the same no matter who felt it. He knew the love of parents for their children was the same no matter who experienced it. He knew hunger was the same and so on. Simply put, he cared and would dedicate every waking moment to making the world the place it should have been long, long ago.

People endured war, ecological destruction, killer air pollution, rising sea levels, grinding poverty, and intractable lifelong debt that billions could never repay. Religious fundamentalism—Christian, Muslim, Hindu, Jewish, Orthodox, and more—became a solace for many in lieu of better options that most true believers had never bothered to even search for, as they turned to outmoded, clearly delusional made up stories in desperation, given the bleakness of their current predicaments and the widespread human carnage distributed across the world.

Lucky Jason stepped off the plane into Pacifica, a utopian reality built by fellow humans who knew that if a paradise was anywhere, it should be for everyone—not just the lucky few.

He kept asking why *he*, among so many billions of fellow humans, had the good fortune of starting life over on Pacifica. Despite the guilt, he repeatedly transformed it into a force for good. As his role in changing the world grew, each bit of guilt gradually dissolved into nothingness.

From the first second the plane's door was opened by the barefoot pilot in his tie-dyed shirt and shorts, beads hanging from his tanned neck, Jason knew he had arrived. The first breath he took was not just the cleanest air he had ever breathed, but it was infused with the most beautiful fragrance in the world, the unmistakable ambrosia-like scent of the ubiquitous frangipani trees across Tofua. These smooth-barked gifts from Mother Nature offered an unparalleled gift to the olfactory senses of the humans who came anywhere near them. There simply was no other smell, no other titillating nose candy, quiver-inducing offering quite like it. The Pacificans recognized this early and imported over a million saplings to complement the existing frangipani trees that naturally sprouted on Tofua, transforming the once-obscure island into the single most hope-inducing place on the face of the planet.

Jason trod carefully down the few steps leading from the plane onto the tarmac, made from reusable, locally sourced clay and dead coral that they crushed and combined into a mixture that hardened quickly in the tropical sun and only required re-grading once a year. Far better than the earth-destroying bitumen and concrete that now disgustingly covered huge portions of the planet, killing each and every microbe, these surfaces preserved life. Mama Nature had struck back—and struck back hard—against the horrible humans who had collectively raised their shared middle finger and silently muttered, "Fuck you, Mother Earth. Fuck you, Mother Nature. Fuck you, fellow humans who have fallen under the spell of this 'we're all connected delusion.' Fuck all of you. We see, we take, we process, we use, we discard, and we start all over again. And if it means the end of our species, then so be it. The ride was a mighty fine one, and on we'll plunder and procure until there's nothing left…"

He stepped onto the firm, life-infused soil and scanned the welcoming committee that greeted each arriving plane, picking out the familiar faces of his new family. These psychedelic love warriors had given up on the rest of the world for now to build something so original, so new, so innovative that, once known, would shock everyone.

He could hear the first notes of the perfect sitar raga welcoming guests to Pacifica in the background when he first saw Amber, then

Nathan, then Horst, Flea, Dr. Julia, and all the others. There were smiles all around, hugs in abundance, the sharing of kisses and gifts, happiness, and delight.

They walked to the small terminal, completely covered by plants, vines, and at least fifty varieties of flowers, as well as edible herbs and other green bushes. Despite feeling overjoyed at his good fortune, a smidgen of deep fear lingered. Like every other utopian attempt—even those simply dreamed up in books and stories—Pacifica might eventually fail once the initial enthusiasm wore off, egos finally took hold, internal conflict between the purists and the realists arose, and the rest of the world felt too threatened by the alternative Pacifica offered, finding ways to end it before it became the political destiny of ever-growing numbers of people across all the continents.

But for the moment, in this brief snippet of cosmic time, everyone who was anyone wanted to ride the wave that was Pacifica. This societal culmination of decades of planning was deeply grounded in the wisdom of sages, rather than the individualistic and selfish lunatics that swayed the grotesque political classes. It was a truly divine place, free from all of the problems that beset other countries—to one degree or another.

But it was neither the magic, the mushrooms, nor some sort of new religion that made all of this possible. It wasn't the billions upon billions of dollars that had been made available either. No, it was much more the case that the *zeitgeist* had combined with the latest advances in the world of IT and tech and an overwhelming feeling by ever more people that something new had to be done to save humanity. Simply put, the Industrial Age, capitalism, inequality, environmental destruction, war, the arms industry, and obesity were essentially all the same thing. It was time for those who saw beyond superficial differences—the humans who grasped the oneness of things—who treated all humans as one family, to finally do something, do anything, to get this incredible species back on track. The world had surely lost its way, and nothing, it seemed, even Jason's powerful speeches and work in the corridors of power, could set it right.

To his left, he heard someone shout, "Hey, Jason, great fucking speech, man! We replayed it yesterday morning right after *Interstellar* on the island sound system, and everyone loved it! And believe me, they'll show their love in ways you will not believe… and I mean that in only the best sense of the term."

Jason smiled his biggest grin yet, and deep within his being he silently said, just to himself, *I'm home. At last, I'm home*.

Viva Pacifica Viva!

40

The Pacificans were not just clever every so often; they were brilliant all of the time. They knew history deeply. Unlike most, they learned from it. They explored every political theory ever developed, every single body politic ever brought into existence, every strand of every ideology to see what worked, what didn't, and what might be the next step in humanity's political evolution. This place would not become a Burning Man 2.0, a fake new capital city like Canberra, Nay Pyi Daw, or Arusha, or anything like that odd wall of a metropolis being built in the Middle East. It had absolutely nothing to do with the new town those Silicon Valley guys were building in California. No, far from it. Beyond the political, social, and economic marvels that made Pacifica famous, the truly revolutionary developments were in their energy policies and practices.

Though you couldn't find the presence of a very active volcano on Horst's to-do list, the ever-present, angry lava-laden earth-crust belcher was viewed not as a threat to be feared, but rather as a potential source of permanent, clean, and *easy-to-capture* energy. On top of that they would produce *easy-to-store* energy to fuel the world's cleanest society and most sustainable economy.

No, it was much more than that. This would be added to the list of inspirational advances by this strange band of merry world changers. They had seen enough of the harm caused by the BilliBros and the cruel system that fuelled their wealth, so they harnessed every gram of their collective minds—what they called the One Mind or Hive Mind

—toward one successful experiment after another.

The Pacificans were anything but lazy slouches. They worked incredibly hard, not out of coercion but driven by a shared desire to prove that a new way of doing things was possible, realistic, and doable. They knew that if they succeeded on Tofua and Kao, they would set the target for all other places that equally wished to create a new way of doing things. Most Pacificans rose with the sun, or earlier, and spent a solid hour or more exercising or meditating. After a delicious tropical breakfast of fruit, berries, nuts, freshly baked multigrain muffins, and other delights, off they would go to work. This society did not demand worker loyalty in exchange for a paycheck. Yes, they were paid in whichever currency they preferred, including the crypto option, but money was beside the point for most of them.

They believed money was really only valuable to two groups: those with none or too little, and those with too much—who just wanted more. The people of Pacifica had mostly transcended the money addiction long ago, each in their own individual ways. Unlike the billionaires of the world, they simply had the wisdom to say, "I have enough; I need no more…" once they reached a certain level of net worth. For the majority, however, it was more a question of nothing less than life's true meaning.

When people sought community, compassion, clean air, pure food, simplicity, excellent health, and an occasional mushroom trip, the whole idea of money seemed obscene. The capitalists and even the communist capitalists had convinced the world that happiness rested in things, in consumption, in greed, in plastic, in new things, in throwing things "away," in competing with one's neighbors for prestige, in brand awareness, never wanting less, always wanting more. And, for a long time, it had worked. That ideology of a cancer cell, where the sole objective is to divide and grow, dominated every country and virtually every family in one or more ways. As more and more people finally understood that they shared a single, finite, priceless planet, the more aware among them began to change. The pursuit of material possessions fell by the wayside.

The Pacificans knew that a human life was exceptionally fleeting. On average, people live less than thirty thousand days, eat less than one hundred thousand meals, and spend one-third of their time sleeping. They set out to use this limited time not to be a cog in capital's wheel but to squeeze every drop out of it that they can. Meditating for an hour or two is worth more than three hours many spent commuting daily. Exercising for an hour is worth more than a lunch break in a canteen with horrible food and an equally horrible environment. Art beats factory work hands down. Music beats a life in retail by a mile. Social responsibility beats individual effort without question. And compassion beats competition all the way.

Horst and Flea had set the parameters for Pacifica and had drawn up plans for walking paths, landscaping, housing plots, agriculture, and all the rest. When the first ten thousand began arriving, the basics were in place, thanks to the handy Tongans who worked just as hard. Upon disembarking at either the port or landing strip, newcomers were greeted with flower garlands and offerings of coconut milk and sweet treats. Residents would quickly register them and based on their wishes, allocate either a small home in one of the exquisite bamboo multi-occupancy buildings or a housing plot where they could build their own home.

Many people were surprised and even shocked that Pacifica worked at all. After the countless failures of other intentional communities built from scratch, particularly the famous hippy communes of the 1960s and 1970s, which seemed almost without exception to have faded into oblivion, everyone who knew about this experiment predicted it, too, would fail. But it didn't. In fact, it flourished, becoming the beacon of hope that its founders had always hoped it would be. Pacifica had become more than just a place. It was an idea whose time had come.

More than that, mini-Pacificas began popping up all over the place. Sometimes a single suburban street would begin calling itself Pacifica and proudly fly *Viva Pacifica Viva* flags from their street signs. Other times, entire cities sometimes proclaimed themselves allies of Pacifica and, with grants from the original Pacifica, built their own locally determined versions. Chiang Mai, Thailand was one of the first cities to adopt the Pacifica way, followed by Santa Fe, New Mexico in the United States, Amsterdam, Bali, and Pondicherry in India, to name just a few. Everyone who wished to would take the "Pacifica Promise," then set off to build the next version of that singular place, which had given billions across the planet hope for a better tomorrow after so many decades of hopelessness.

No one had ever really tried to tunnel into a volcano to collect and control some of the infinite supplies of molten-powered energy, but the creative and risk-taking Pacificans did. They discovered that by digging two tunnels in the right place at the right time, they could safely channel lava into the ocean while releasing only heat and steam through the other tunnel, which quickly helped Pacifica become energy self-sufficient.

Using lava as an energy source amazed many, but the small size of the drilled hole particularly surprised them. A thirty-centimeter-wide hole generated enough power to fuel the turbines of this new ecological land, energized by an incredible combination of alternative energy, hardworking, and wisdom-laden Bodhisattva citizens, quarterly mushroom celebrations, and a shared vision: unify and embrace oneness, or perish down the toilet bowl of history, swirling into the drain of doom where the human experiment will end with a single stinky flush.

They not only set up a series of invisible collectors of wave energy and tidal differential energy sources along the more deserted parts of the coastline that provided additional energy, but they were also working on a fusion project to push things along as well.

Ubiquitous solar panels, solar paint, and solar cubes covered every structure in view. They had placed several highly efficient windmills on the windiest parts of the island. Pacifica collected all waste, both human and non-human in derivation, as if it were gold, and processed it into a large biomass factory to produce gas for emergencies, used only when necessary.

At all other times, night and day, Pacifica was not just energy self-sufficient but so clean, so pure, so free from any sort of nasty emissions, especially CO^2 or methane, that it had by far the best climate change policy of any community on Earth. All other things being equal, if nothing changed and the rest of the planet left Pacifica alone, this new nation could go on forever without a single oil tanker from the Middle East, a gas ship from Australia, or coal from anywhere ever arriving on its shores. At successive COP meetings where global climate policy was hammered out (usually with little effect), the phrase “Yes, it will be difficult, but Pacifica did it and so can we” became increasingly common.

41

They varied the enclosure's temperature to emulate different climates, ensuring the five stars of *Los Cincos* never knew where they were. Most importantly, they offered an incredibly diverse diet with the cuisines changing by the day. It could be Indian on Monday, then West African on Tuesday. Wednesday brought Italian, Thursday Swedish, and then Friday was Mexican. No pattern. Always random. The cooks made their selections from a lottery of over five hundred dishes every day or two, creating an exquisite culinary repertoire. None of the five would go hungry any time soon, that is for certain.

Sometimes they would give the smallest of clues and serve locally grown mangos to the five as a healthy, vitamin-rich breakfast. But far from calming them down by enabling them to enjoy one of nature's truly divine flavors, such things often just resulted in the BilliBros arguing with one another as they were already so prone to do.

The bickering began almost from the first moment they awoke from their respective week-long slumbers, each of them wallowing in a state of distinct befuddlement at the insanity of it all. Predictably, each of the five muttered, "Where am I?" as they re-entered life. As their eyes adjusted and they began their initial recons of the place, one after the other, in various languages, all called out variations of "What the hell is this? Hello? Hello! Is anyone here?"

Jasper awoke first, and once he got his bearings, *anger* hardly described his state of mind. Helmut was next.

"Like, what the fucking hell… what is this place? It is, like, so *povo*."

Then Harry, followed by Lawrence, and finally William.

In what became arguably the long-running show's most satisfying moment, all five stars simultaneously realized they were not only incarcerated but trapped under the same impermeable roof as their four mortal enemies. The collective shock was almost visible to the show's early subscribers. *Los Cincos* went live thirty-six hours before the captives awoke, and the news went viral within seconds. As a result, 450 million people had subscribed within a day and a half, clearly entranced by the thought that people were finally fighting back against *the* scourge.

For more than fifteen minutes, the five billionaires sat in complete silence, trying to figure out what was happening, where they were, and, most of all, how to escape.

"Hey, Harry, what the fuck is this, man?" asked Puhler. "Did you arrange this? Is this the prelude to a party or something?"

"Or a fuck fest?" Jasper tastelessly added, unable to help himself. It dawned on all of them rather quickly, however, that they had been kidnapped, that they were being held captive against their will, and that escape would not be easy.

"This is just so unfair!" Eijkelje screamed. "After all I have done to provide weapons for those who need them!"

"Yeah," Larry chimed in, "I invented a drink that satisfied India's thirst and then the world, and they chose to do this to a good guy like me! Fuck that!"

Viewers ate it up, and more and more people signed up to watch as much as possible. The first week went by with a series of countless questions posed by one BilliBro prisoner to another. The real arguments began in just ten days, all starting over food.

"Fuck you, Harry, you were always the greediest motherfucker of all. I gave you my mangos three days in a row. Now you refuse to keep your promise and try again for mango number four. You're not getting it, you twit."

Harry endured yet another word blast from Lawrence, who was still, all these years later, suffering the lingering edges of his dual addiction to both Quench and the evil anti-opiate medicine E-Z Quit that he'd marketed. The King of Addiction felt it, and it felt—most decidedly—anything but groovy.

Jasper mostly moped around and avoided interacting with others, while Puhler and Schwanzkopf, perhaps due to their European origins, acted out their own personal version of World War III almost hourly. This brought tremendous glee to the now over two billion viewers glued to their screens, watching these evil men fight in a closed world none of them really understood.

They were all glad to be alive, of course, their feelings of self-importance and ego-driven delusions of grandeur still very much ever-present, despite their new experience of incarceration, but a constant sense of universal confusion overwhelmed them, making escape seem completely unviable to those who had considered it.

Little did they know, escape was even more impossible than they imagined. Isolated on an unpopulated island in the central Pacific, they were trapped by four perimeter fences, internal steel walls, hundreds of sensors, and an impermeable structure with meter-thick walls. This made their prison more secure than most super-max facilities in the once-great United States, which now wobbled on its knees.

As the effects of climate change worsened, as debt levels became far beyond unsustainable, as the US dollar lost its shine and primacy, the markets had crashed, property values plummeted, and the always-poor infrastructure had worsened to levels normally associated with places like the Central African Republic or Chad. After delaying the payments owed to the piper for far too long, the never-satiated, materialistic Americans had finally, once and for all, shot themselves in the foot one too many times, and the place that had once held out so much hope for the world had become both ungovernable and unforgiving. China had tried to take advantage of this long demise, but they, too, had totally failed in this quest, not realizing that people actually like freedom more than social credit scores, constant surveillance, and re-education camps, not to mention the failed attempts at hegemony that only led the rest of the world to despise the once great Chinese Communist Party, which was now a shrivelled version of its earlier self, with only the most loyal still holding on to its very own authoritarian addictions.

It was this dual demise of both superpowers, empires in waning, that brought so much hope to the ways of life people witnessed in Pacifica. Pacifica *was* the way forward, a place *and* an idea of promise. It was the future. Nation-states, one and all, were vestiges of history, well past their prime, and now widely seen by ever-growing numbers of people as the primary reason for the world's problems. Which, together with the grotesque ways of the billionaire class, had brought the whole world to its knees.

A new dawn was coming, a new start on the verge of emergence, and if it was up to Nathan, Jason, Amber, Horst, Flea, Dr. Julia, and all the millions of others who backed them, it would be Pacifica itself that provided at least a modicum of hope that the new world being built on the old would, for once, actually be something so much better than people could have ever imagined. There would no longer be empires, nation-states, billionaires, or dictators. The world would be an ecological and egalitarian democracy through and through.

In addition, on the positive side of the ledger, there would be no poverty, no lack of access to medicine, no forced displacement, no conflicts, no discrimination, and no fear or hatred. Humanity's true potential for good would finally be unleashed with consequences that would change the species forever into what it was somehow meant to be: a life form of self-reflective consciousness, capable of self-actualization, enlightenment, where everyone lived selfless lives of compassion and mercy, where kindness and gentleness emerged freely and easily, where love and lust were shared among all, where psychedelic medicines were as plentiful as the biodynamic fruits and vegetables that grew everywhere so abundantly. This was a place without hate crimes. The only crime was when people didn't love enough—and that is what they called a "love crime."

The capitalistic fantasy world that had dominated since the dawn of the Industrial Era had petered out to an inglorious end, having given much, for sure, but also having created the conditions for its own demise and that of the planet itself. People were tired of it. They were sickened and angry. They were desperate for something new, and the increasingly obvious answer was Pacifica.

They would finally implement Gandhi's credo: "There is enough for everyone's need, but not enough for everyone's greed." They had learned the lessons of failed revolutions across the ages, the failures of what was called "communism," but which, in fact, it never really was, and the evils of ethnically-based hatred, which seemed to pop up again and again just as the last bout of madness was coming to its natural and exhausting end.

42

All of this contributed to the reasons why viewer numbers grew so quickly. The show had become so popular, in fact, that even if people knew the world's most-watched 24/7 reality show—viewed by billions of paying subscribers—was controlled and produced by the same people behind Pacifica, they'd still prefer living in the island society over their current lives. Even if they knew they were watching a crime in progress, a growing majority was on Pacifica's side. And yet, as if a miracle, no one had yet put two and two together. No one – other than the minds in which the idea was hatched – knew where *Los Cincos* was being filmed. Not a single soul.

People placed ever-larger bets on what would happen during the next twenty-four hours. It was so ubiquitous that most people simply called it LC. On any given day, on any given street, you could approach any given person—be it on a thoroughfare in Ohio, a backstreet in Osaka, a desert road in Oman, or a seaside café in Oslo—and they would not only know about the show but also share unsolicited opinions on the captives and where they believed they were being held.

With subscriptions costing only one hundred USD a year in the Global North (less than 30 cents a day for this!), and only ten dollars a year in the Global South, it brought in billions of dollars for Pacifica after the funds had been re-routed 25 times or more through a series of shell companies making tracing impossible. *Use their tools against them.* These funds simply added to their increasingly large financial reserves. To this day, no one knows if the five people whose lives were observed in such detail for so long ever realized they were being broadcast to billions. The cameras, perfectly emulating ordinary CCTV security cameras, had kept them unaware—but the world certainly knew. With the global repulsion at the world's billionaires, people watched and watched and watched.

Families argued over which of the BilliBros was the nicest, who was the meanest, the cutest, the ugliest, and the most stylish. People across the world claimed to have met one of the five and promised that "they were really nice." Women looking for a rich husband would watch for days on end, trying to figure out every character trait of each of these vile men just in case they survived the ordeal, making plans to grab one of them for their big bank balances, not realizing just yet, of course, that they might not be as large as they had assumed.

Viewers didn't always care about new shoes or new iPhones or new consumer products of any sort. But don't try to take away access to *Los Cincos*, for if you did, then you would see a real global revolution come about overnight, no doubt about it. The people might not be addicted to Quench anymore, but they were definitely addicted to LC.

What did all those addicted billions love so much about *Los Cincos*? Was it that they were watching a crime in progress? Did they finally want Robin Hood to win after decades of his kindly and well-intentioned, yet unsuccessful, attempts at wealth transfer, no matter how justified Mr. Hood's efforts may have been? Or was it perhaps simply the excitement of watching imprisoned people, surfing the wave of internal fear that it so easily could have been them, were circumstances different than they were?

These are all partially right, but what really kept eyes glued to the screen more than anything else was the bird's eye view—up as close as possible—into the clearly disturbed minds of these billionaires, where pathos, paranoia, and pettiness oozed like the lava of the nearby volcano for all the world to see. These five were such awful human beings that probably none of the more than two billion people (and counting) who were watching so breathlessly wanted to be anything like these insecure men.

These tragic souls, already mentally anguished before their incarceration, all direly needed psychological assistance. Without it, they would clearly never have enough money, enough power, or enough dominance. They would amass more with each passing day, up until the very day of their deaths—never satisfied, never satiated, never able to be content with what they had, never happy with their possessions, nor their existence and the knowledge that they would never have to work again, never have to lift a finger, never even have to eat with the same fork on the same plate—or even the same table—again.

The world watched psychopathy play out before their very eyes. It terrified them, but they were riveted too. People just couldn't look away.

The BilliBros had used and thrown away, used and thrown away, used and thrown away. They had burned more oil, used more gas, consumed more, eaten more, drunk more, pissed more, shit more, and fucked everything that moved. Ah, the wonderfully enlightened minds of the BilliBros—all on show for the whole world to see up close and more personal than all of the viewers had ever seen. Many had suspected they were horrible but not quite as horrible as this.

During one night's ramblings, for instance, Ness and Puhler were at each other's throats again, each blaming the other for their internment.

"It's your fault, Harry, you fuckwit. If you weren't such a prick and been so public about it, maybe we could have gone on our merry and largely secret ways! We could've fucked society in the proverbial ass and glided along in whatever form of Earth-destroying vehicle we wanted. No one would have bothered us, and we could have kept on pulling strings with the political leaders who we put into place to protect our riches as we always have. But no, you—yes, YOU—just had to go on *Fox News* in that fucking interview with that white supremacist. That turned the world not only against you but against all of us, you FUCKER!"

He lost control, and if Jasper hadn't jumped in—much to everyone's relief—the latest brawl would likely have ended in the death of one of these ghoulish creeps, though it would have seemed no great loss to humanity. But the Dutch guy jumped in, likely motivated more by the fear of losing twenty-five percent of the assholes he was interned with, leaving fewer people to mock. And so the fight ended in a draw, as they always did, while the world watching this spectacle voted once again. Normal people: 1. Billionaires: 0.

If you listened closely enough, no matter where you were in the world, you could undoubtedly hear the chants of "Killionaire! Killionaire! We are the Killionaire!"

The ordinary citizens of the world—priceless, irreplaceable, normal people who deserved so much more than the current political and economic system could offer—finally understood that there was no single Killionaire. No, everyone had a role in killing the very idea that any individual should ever amass a billion dollars or more, let alone hundreds of billions—and certainly not a trillion. This sickness had to end.

43

"How many times do I have to say it? We are NOT killing any of them. We are not going to create another Reign of Terror, no matter how easy it would be to do so. What kind of people do you think we are? Can you imagine how we would be seen by the millions of people who already hate Pacifica if anyone ever found out what we were up to?" Nathan sternly yelled at Jason, rejecting his suggestion that death was the only thing good enough, not just for the five they were holding —but every last one of the BilliBros, wherever they were.

"That Stalin wannabe kills them right and left and always seems to get away with it. So why shouldn't we? A lot of asshole leaders throughout history—and a fair number of those alive today—have killed their opponents and gotten away with it. Why can't we?" he demanded.

"No one even knows who the Killionaire is. They are totally confused. Those idiots think it's some serial killer doing the rounds, planning to off them one by one. No one has any clue. They never will if we keep our mouths shut, which we will. Am I correct, my friend?"

"Of course, you know you can trust us. No matter how long they threaten, torture, or incarcerate me, I will never talk. I know the others won't either. This will be our secret to keep until we die. But wouldn't it be OK if we find a way to tell our kids, so they can tell the mystery to the world—after the last of us passes on back into the ether?"

"That's not a bad idea, man. How about we all prepare notes for our kids now and agree—at this very moment—that whoever lives the longest gives their note to their kids? They can decide whether or not to spill the beans, but at least they'll know we made things happen on a grandiose scale."

The founders of Pacifica were deeply unsettled by the thought that its immense success and the promise it fulfilled, time and again, were at least partly induced by a serious crime. And yet, they always doubted whether any of it would have been possible had they not had the courage and the means to carry it out so successfully.

Who would have imagined that fellow humans—as they reluctantly concurred them to be—like William Puhler, Harold Ness, Jasper Eijkelje, Helmut Schwanzkopf, and Larry Lawson could be so easily taken and placed onto Kao without anyone on the planet knowing their location except the Killionaire? Just months ago, Eijkelje was on his mega yacht, intentionally infecting women with incurable venereal diseases. Now, he's incarcerated on a tropical island, a turn of events beyond the possibility of anyone's imagination.

But so it was. Five alpha males—ego-driven, greedy, selfish billionaires—were nestled together like peas in a pod in a climate-controlled, luxurious center, fighting for dominance and bragging rights while the rest of the world watched from the edge of their seats. How wonderful but how horrible all at once, yin and yang confusedly intermingling with no possibility of returning to their respective sides, now or ever.

But none of this mattered, for what was done was done. No one could deny that, as glorious as it was, Pacifica was built on a series of serious crimes—a felony within a felony, surrounded by yet another felony—all conceived, carried out, and coordinated by three of the finest humans to ever live—three people who had never committed another offense other than the smallest of infractions, mostly related to drug use, on a planet rapidly reconsidering the absurdity of prohibition. And it niggled and niggled and niggled away inside each of them.

These pure, compassionate, sublime people who loved everyone—well, just about everyone—more than they loved themselves, and who loved the planet and the miracle of life it created and allowed to exist even more than that. These three humans with their three hearts, their three brains, their six lungs, and six eyes and ears and arms and legs, their miles of veins and arteries, their billions of cells, and all the rest, shared a worldview that had thought everything through, grounded in the knowledge that life was worth preserving, life was everything, and yet…

Just as they had intended all along, the world got it wrong, as it so often had. It presumed that *the* Killionaire was a single person rather than an *idea* implemented by the multi-headed organism that formed the core founders of Pacifica, proof of systems theory where the sum of the whole is greater than its parts. The real Killionaire, of course, leaked a false story to the media, suggesting that some lunatic, probably somewhere in the US, the land of serial killers, was the culprit. From the start, the Killionaire was never a single person. The Killionaire was Pacifica, an ideal society tainted by its criminal origins —not just as a model psychedelic society but as an enterprise that turned to crime to change the world. The debate—between those who wanted to kill and those who only wanted to kill the very notion of flourishing billionairism—threatened to destroy the Pacifica dream long before it became the haven for the lucky few who chose the highest possible quality of life.

For a rocky period the arguments between Amber, Jason, and Nathan often nearly boiled over into violence, with coalitions forming, then quickly dissolving, as they debated whether or not killing should be part of their plan. The non-violent, people-loving group prevailed, and all others quickly joined the majority. And so the "killing" became purely metaphorical. No one would be even threatened with any sort of physical violence, but keeping the word as a rallying cry within their movement would remain.

44

The Killionaire concept was a stroke of genius. As long as no one knew they would never kill anyone, let alone their BilliBro guests, the mere public linguistic linkages between the words 'kill' and 'billionaire' would take on a life of its own, in effect preparing the world for a time when such a thing as a billionaire did not and could not exist at all.

But all of this would mean nothing if their secret got out and they were exposed. So far—at least as far as they knew—no one had even the slightest clue that *Los Cincos* were being held by the Pacificans on Pacifica. To keep their secret, Nathan and friends had developed an exceptionally complex series of measures to distract, trick and confuse law enforcement agencies and private eyes across the world. All it would take was a single witness, a lone piece of evidence pointing in their direction, and the world's most popular crime would be exposed. Were this to occur, everything that Pacifica stood for and their aims to eradicate extreme wealth would come to naught.

With their hundreds of inside connections of Pacifica supporters in Interpol and various national and local police departments, the Pacificans would hear relatively quickly if their crime had been compromised. Until now, almost two years into it, any links between *Los Cincos* and Pacifica, however, remained pure conjecture; simple guess work and hunches by sleuths both real and supposed. Theories about who had kidnapped the BilliBros and why, as well as determining just where it was that they were being held, occupied the minds of many as nightly news broadcasts and interview shows became increasingly obsessed with finding answers.

One theory that seemed to be gaining some traction was that the BilliBros were being held somewhere within the confines of one of their very own isolated compounds. There were hundreds of these potential locations spread across the face of the planet. During the first year of the project, intensive searches were carried out every week or two in all of these bastions of extreme wealth. The authorities searched *Winner* and found nothing. They searched Larry's building in Mumbai to no avail, and they spent considerable time looking around Puhler's estate in Patagonia, as well as the bolt hole in southern New Zealand. But other than interviews with potential witnesses, these searches turned up nothing of any import.

There were leads and there were clues, but these, too, ended up with nothing to show for them, even after resource-intensive wild goose chases that always seemed promising until it was abundantly clear that there was no reason for such optimism. What those within law enforcement didn't know, of course, was that—as always—the Pacificans had planned everything rather well. The secret ingredient within their larger secret, of course, were the highly useful roles played by their favorite accomplices—Nicole, Ra, Cedric and Eddie. Iene had already sailed off into the distant sunset and was living an isolated and calm life in Bali after her final voyage on *Ream Machine* all those months ago. She needed distance and peace and quiet, and she got it. But the roles played by the other four assistants were vital spokes in the wheel of their plan. They had already, of course, played indispensable roles in getting their respective BilliBro into positions whereby they could easily be transferred onto planes first and then onto the yacht for transport to Kao. In those tasks, they had performed majestically and flawlessly. Since those initial successes, however, they had carried out a series of smokescreens designed to confuse and frustrate law enforcement. Every few days, they would plant false stories on the internet, the vast majority of which became conspiracy theories believed by millions of small-minded conspiracists, and none of which had anything at all to do with truth. In the Age of Conspiracy, such methods were almost fool proof.

One of the false leads, planted by Eddie, focused on creating the impression of a massive digital broadcast center in Serbia from where he would claim—using a false identity—that unusual massive energy bursts were occurring with increased strength and regularity. These bursts, he claimed on the phone to local police while using voice alteration technology, could indicate that this rural location was where *Los Cincos* were being held. He planted the same story on numerous conspiracy websites, and within minutes the made-up story went viral and all attention was placed on rural Serbia, a location about as far as possible from the true location of the kidnapped BilliBros. This story, just like all of their made-up tales, required thousands of person-hours, countless police and law enforcement officials, weeks and weeks of news media coverage and more—precisely what the Pacificans had wished to occur.

After all the false leads had been checked with nothing turning up, weeks would pass, sometimes months, and those seeking the location of the five BilliBros would have to admit it was no clearer than before.

All told, the assistants put out dozens of fake stories to keep the eyes of authority away from Kao. And it worked. Every single time. Some of these were so simple that it amazed them that such trickery could confuse even the most sophisticated government intelligence agencies. Others were more complex, and in internal discussions within the Pacifican core who knew all the details, the best of the lot was the operation they labelled as *Les Cinq*. They just laughed their hearts out when they came up with this idea and laughed even more when it became self-evident that law enforcement and the public at large fell for it hook, line and sinker.

The *Les Cinq* plan involved five life-loving Frenchmen who gathered at an isolated farmhouse near the French mountain town of Chamonix and who re-created an almost perfect facsimile of what they could see while watching *Los Cincos*. The assembled five men each resembled one of the five BilliBros, and with make-up applied judiciously enough, on camera they looked remarkably similar. The same applied to the room in which they found themselves, which was designed to almost perfectly emulate the room the world was watching 24/7 on their screens.

Once all the ingredients of the deception were in place, they began filming and intentionally overloading the electricity grid every hour on the hour just to create suspicions. On a selected day, they put more than twenty hours of footage on YouTube, which amassed tens of millions of views within hours. Law enforcement officials began viewing these, examining electricity burst reports and then triangulated the likely location of *Les Cinq*, which they still believed were *Los Cincos*. This again diverted attention and resources, and after another wasted eight weeks, those seeking the kidnapped BilliBros were back at square one.

The amount of time and energy the Pacificans had spent on protecting their secret was clearly paying off. Every few weeks, a new distraction was developed, people fell for it and spent more weeks deluding themselves into thinking: "Finally, we've solved the crime." The same applied on Kao itself, where Horst had ensured that the world's most advanced encryption measures were in place and functioning perfectly. He also ensured that a combination of VPN networks, firewalls and unique uses of artificial intelligence all contributed to immediately diverting any effort to find the site source of where *Los Cincos* were being held. The delay that was built into the never-ending broadcasting of the show meant that any real-time search as to the source was destined to fail.

And so it went. Month after month, as the BilliBros got used to their confinement, billions of viewers became ever more addicted to the "Show of Shows," as many were referring to it now. Even more importantly, the world's governments and political classes began more seriously than ever to discuss whether the time was right to tackle billionairism once and for all.

45

"Jasper, remember that time when you took me out in your boat and those lovely Danish beauties joined us aboard *Ream Machine*? I wonder what happened to them?" Puhler asked his fellow inmate.

"Who the fuck cares?" replied the disgusting Dutchie.

Puhler began noticing some strange physical changes in and on his body since finding himself the unknowing star of a show watched by billions. But he had yet to ponder what they might be.

"Willi, my boy," Jasper replied with a sly smirk on his face, "there have been so many over the years, that even my masterful mind and its miraculous memory skills find it difficult now to sort them all out from one another. Without my trusty journal at hand, it's really impossible to say. It's all one big pussy to me these days." He chortled, noticing red spots on his leg, remarkably similar to those appearing on Puhler's body.

"Hey, wait a minute, Eijkelje. What's that red thing on your leg?"

Jasper looked down to see an ugly crimson lesion on his left calf, which did, indeed, immediately start to worry him. At first, he thought it might just be yet another skin cancer to have burned off if he was ever to see a doctor again. But then, as he looked more closely, terror struck him right where it mattered.

Holy fuck, he thought. *That's a sign of AIDS. I finally got fucking AIDS after all those years of keeping my HIV at bay and a secret from all those unsuspecting goddesses I gave it to. And double holy fuck, it looks a lot like that thing on Puhler's neck.* He started to shake with the realization, much to the delight of the billions of viewers watching this all unfold. Right then, both men shared the beguiling satori moment: during their rancid little boat ride, Jasper had given Puhler HIV, which had now sadly morphed into full-blown AIDS. The viewers had rarely been so gripped and viewer numbers skyrocketed even further upwards, with headlines on the world's media shouting to the few readers left: "Eijkelje gives Puhler AIDS! Both need medical care!"

Until the fateful night of infection neither man had ever had the pleasure of the other man, and only once in their lives had they "done it" with a fellow male. In the middle of another night of gooey debauchery on *Ream Machine*, there were so many bodies, so many drugs, so much whisky, and so few boundaries that at one moment—when their heads just happened to be near one another in and amongst a throng of women and lubricant—Jasper had told William, "I'm going to fuck your ass, klootzak." For a reason the world may never come to know, William consented, and the Dutch dick probed the Argie's ass in a twisted pain fest that may have given Eijkelje another body shiver while simultaneously giving Puhler the pestilence.

The hatred became palpable as William realized that the man—whom he had considered a friend—had known all along he had HIV. He had likely infected hundreds of women over the years, probably thousands. Now, William Puhler was the latest and only male victim of this horrible man.

"You gave me AIDS, you fucker! You're dead!"

As the realization dawned on both men, Puhler lunged violently at the Dutchman, grabbing his neck with both hands and shouting, "I'm going to kill you, you motherfucker."

Barely able to speak, Eijkelje then managed to say, even more disgustingly, "Motherfucker, you say. Well, I did once procure your mother for orgasmic purposes, you asshole, and she was oh so fine. Into the hole out of which you came, I came too!"

This, of course, enraged his HIV-positive cohort even more, which led to further attempts at strangulation, additional efforts at freeing himself, and various other attempts using legs, hands, arms, shoulders, knees, jaws, heads, and everything else in a vicious effort to push each other to the limits of life. If death ensued, well, so be it. The three other BilliBros, in green jumpsuits covered in dollar signs, stood aside, afraid of getting AIDS from the two fighters. They began yelling at them to give it a rest and chill.

Right about then, on one of the very rare occasions that they heard anything through the loudspeakers placed next to all those cameras recording every move and every sound for all the world to see, a deafening sound projected at maximum volume blasted through the speakers at a level of pitch that floored the two men, ending the brawl immediately. They both went back to their respective corners of the impromptu ring. Then they heard a voice rising over the feedback sounds above them saying, “Go to your rooms. Dr. Julia, the healer, will arrive in thirty minutes to examine all of you.”

46

The BilliBros attentively listened, shocked by the first contact from their captors in weeks, and slightly excited about the prospect of a visitor, even if it was just for medical purposes. Even better yet, it would be a woman, the first and only woman they would see for a long, long time.

They then waited a while, getting over the adrenaline rushes that were coursing through all of their veins, fighters and non-fighters alike, and after precisely thirty minutes, the door opened. In walked Dr. Julia, not in a white coat, not in surgical smocks, not in anything resembling the clothing normally associated with a doctor. Rather, Dr. Julia—master of the mushroom medicine, soul sister to the mushroom mistress Flea, and magical medical miracle worker—entered their involuntary abode wearing a one-piece tie-dyed spandex body sheath covered with imagery and mushrooms. If you looked at it in just the right way and in just the right light, it appeared to make the mushrooms dance and sway as this wisdom-giving medico entered the room with a jar of dark liquid and five small cups, made of bamboo from the nearby forests of Pacifica.

They reluctantly peered from their respective units, which resembled luxurious living rooms more than jail cells. Stocked daily, they were replete with overflowing bowls of fresh tropical fruits, sparkling mineral water, countless teas, organic locally-grown coffee, and a plethora of juices. They were provided every few hours with fresh vegetables, noodles, tofu, seeds, nuts, and a whole array of healthy and nutritious foods to keep the captives alive and well. In fact, they had each reached a level of health none had experienced in years—outside of the AIDS outbreak, that is. All vegan, all the time. The good doctor entered the room, keeping a safe distance and protected by an advanced Pacifican force field designed to keep even the most brutal of potential attackers at bay. She gently informed the not-so-fine gentlemen that their oh-so-fine medicine had arrived.

She carefully placed the cups next to one another and delicately poured equal amounts of the potion into each one until nothing was left in the jar that she had brought with her. She instructed them in the magical arts of successful self-medication with gifts from the Earth and told them that they should each come to the table in alphabetical order based on the first letter of their first name, grab a cup, drink it in one gulp, place the empty cup back onto the table, and return to their cells. They did this with no sense of force and certainly displayed no opposition to these instructions, as one by one they came forward, drank the brown fluid, and returned peacefully to their cells to await further instruction.

Once they were all sitting in their recliner chairs, the places favored by all of them because of the incredible comfort, Dr. Julia calmly and politely said, "Gentlemen, thank you for so peacefully drinking the medicine. This will heal you. This medicine will take you places I cannot even describe in words that will make any sense to you until you have directly experienced it yourselves. This medicine will allow your minds, souls—and especially your spirits—to reach a place you didn't even know existed. But when you arrive, you will recognize it immediately as the place from whence we all came. This medicine will only heal. It will not, indeed, it *cannot*, harm you. Do not fear the medicine."

Helmut blurted out, "I've never seen medicine that looks like that. Like, never. Do you think we're stupid? Do you think we got to where we got by being dumb and stuff?"

Dr. Julia continued, stoically ignoring Helmut's inanity, "Embrace it, accept it, allow it to heal you, and it will. The more you allow, the more it can do. I cannot predict, nor can you or anyone else, precisely what you will experience during the next eight hours. But I can assure you that tomorrow you will see the world in an entirely different way than you have your entire lives, and not in the way of deception or delusion or anything based on fear, but in a way where so much of what has driven you to all think it necessary to become billionaires to prove whatever it is you think you needed to prove will have slipped painlessly away.

"You will all, I promise you, understand why you needed to be here, why your existence as billionaires, or BilliBros—as you once loved to call yourselves—is now finally over forever. Though this may send shivers down your spine now—worry you not, for tomorrow and every day after that you will, for once, be free. You will feel *true* freedom for the very first time, and you will love it. You will enjoy it beyond belief. You will finally understand that *being* beats *doing*, and especially *having*, time and time again. It is *within*… where the true boundless mystery lies, and even more so, where true beauty, and yes, BilliBros, true wealth dwells.

"In just a few minutes, you will see that my words, which now may sound so odd, hold only truth within them. You are not alone, and as long as you are here, you will never be. We will, of course, be watching if there are any problems, as unlikely as this may be. Relax and enjoy. Relax and close your eyes to see what you need to see. Relax and breathe in the life and the love that surrounds us. Relax and merge with the Kosmos. Relax and rejoice as the power of your now irrepressible egos dissolve and free you from their hold. Relax and go *into* and then beyond the Inner Void, the place of true emptiness where you will find everything you could ever need. Relax and grow."

And with that, the delicious doctor left the room, the impenetrable door closing behind her, again locking *Los Cincos* into their shared chamber, where newfound freedom would soon emerge. As the door clicked shut, another click echoed. The other four BilliBros turned to Schwanzkopf, who exclaimed, "Damn, that Dick Chainy even works in here. That, like, totally sucks the big one."

Poor Helmut and his restricted helmet.

47

The world couldn't get enough of watching the BilliBros worm and squirm around their confined shared home, but it was grasping the psychological traumas that these wealth accumulators all seemed to share that fascinated the billions of viewers the most. These five billionaires, and indeed, all the others too, shared the common trait that they simply couldn't trust anyone. Everyone was viewed as a potential foe, a possible thief, a person who was only interested in them because of their money. They had no true friends, lived in constant fear of manipulation, and felt bored with life—given the absence of any need to ever strive for anything. They were never sure what to do with their money when they died, how much—if any—to leave their children, and why they could never be satisfied with the billions they already had. They always wanted more. Always.

There were, of course, a few from the BilliBro clan who understood that true freedom, true joy, true liberation, true self-realization, and the life of a Bodhisattva offered so much more than all those things, all those secret bank accounts, all those boats, all those planes, all those prostitutes, all those golden showers, and all those drugs. A few finally understood the obvious and eventually began withdrawing, giving away their money, a small handful becoming monks and going into permanent retreat in the middle of the woods, living out their days with nothing other than their consciousness, their awareness, their freedom, and their life more than enough to sustain them. But for every one of those, there were hundreds upon hundreds of others who didn't get it and who never would. Their lives were to remain wealthy on the surface, but deeper down they would stay shallow, sad, and anguished as the months rolled into years, all of them deluding themselves into thinking they could take their riches with them after they died but realizing on their deathbeds that there was so much more that they never experienced simply because they were afraid to do so.

Super fans of the show could dismiss the wallowing of the billionaires who kept on earning and acquiring and accumulating year after year. They had real admiration for the tiny fraction of former billionaires who had become spiritual in orientation. But what obsessed them the most was watching *Los Cincos* and seeing the perpetual see-sawing back and forth between those who were trying to accept their fate and letting go of what it meant to once be rich and the others who, even in confinement against their will, couldn't help writing out financial calculations about how much they had made in the previous twenty-four-hour period, even though they had not placed a trade or made a new investment for a good long while.

They were all well versed on the ways of the market, which for the past half-century or more had become entirely skewed in favor of capital over income through work, and basing their calculations on how much money they controlled when they were first kidnapped and their average annual returns, which hovered around twenty-eight percent a year, and a few additions and multiplications later, came to the new number. At one point, Harry yelled out, not realizing that this was extremely far from the present truth, "Hey, fuckers, I made 34.7 million bucks yesterday not lifting a finger, not making a call, not doing anything other than being a prisoner with you four other motherfuckers in some mystery place."

"Who gives a shit, Harry?" said Lawson, the only one of the BilliBros who would seriously consider the path of monkhood if he was ever freed. "We're never going to get to spend it anyway."

It was exchanges such as these that sent the shivers of hate down the spines of the huge viewing audience, many of whose net worth hovered close to the global median, a paltry seven thousand USD. All these billionaires who could make billions a year not even lifting a finger, while most of the world counted a few thousand dollars as everything they had in the entire world—their land, their homes, their tools, their animals, their vehicles, their savings and all the rest. Just seven thousand dollars at the median point of the world's population, meaning billions upon billions of others had far less than that. The world kept on watching for many reasons, but the growing global understanding of just how obscene the net worth of billionaires was, kept them viewing more than just about anything else.

48

Although drugs of all types were very much a core part of the lives of billionaires the world over, including the five now living on the lovely island of Kao, none of *Los Cincos* had ever entered the unique realms of psychedelia. They had overdone just about every white powder drug ever invented, especially coke, and consumed swimming pool quantities of single malt whisky and other worthless forms of destructive, liver-destroying alcohol. All had taken anti-depressants for decades, been addicted to sugar since birth, and generally never strayed too close to either sobriety or even moderation. The champagne had flowed endlessly at the huge, raucous parties where debauchery and exploitation had reigned. Martinis had been part and parcel of business meetings. They had drunk beer for breakfast, as the effects of the previous evenings had lingered—like unwanted groupies around a declining rock star.

They soon learned that lumping together substances with vastly different effects under the term "drugs" was more misleading than any legal status associated with their use, whether good or bad. Grouping soul-destroying crystal meth with LSD was absurd to anyone who knew the difference. Yes, one could describe a meal at Soma as "food," just as one could define a Burger King drive-through meal using the same word, but who in their right mind could possibly group together two such dramatically dissimilar experiences with the word "food." It is very much the same with the term "drugs."

The Pacificans knew this more than most, and Dr. Julia even more so. They rarely used the word "drugs." They used the far more accurate terms of "psychedelics" and, increasingly, "medicine." They knew well, from decades of experience and likely over ten thousand psychedelic trips between them, that language can't adequately describe the places reached through mushrooms, acid, MDMA, DMT, or other psychedelics—so strange, so divine, so real and yet so deeply unlike anything in the "normal" world. They repeated time and time again that "the map is not the territory," but even this phrase falls far short of a lucky user's experience.

In one way or another, usually in the most profound of ways, taking psychedelics changes people and their views of the world, nature, fellow humans, and the universe itself. Those willing to take the leap into the psychedelic realms need immense courage and a willingness to accept whatever it is that the medicine presents for them to ponder. This was no escape from reality or an effort to make things fuzzy and take the edge off. No, this was diving into a dark body of water on a starless, moonless night, trusting that the water would soothe, replenish, and revive the jumper, transforming him or her into a better person than the courageous one who took the initial dive.

They had seen it time and time and time again: the transformational power of psychedelics, particularly the naturally occurring psilocybin in the sacred mushrooms that Flea produced. They somehow shot people through a birth canal of existence into realms of an infinite Inner Void, enabling them to emerge calmer, kinder, and more understanding.

All the original Pacificans had their own tripping stories, and if there was a single thread that connected them all, it was their very own personal experiences with what they universally referred to as *the medicine*. It had prevented disease, cured seemingly incurable illnesses, and built the foundations of lives that combined balanced minds, expanded souls, and spirits, which merged as much with one another as with the very life force itself.

Those who had fearlessly delved into the gifts of the massless, colorless, indescribable, and infinite Inner Void of the eternal abyss found these realities to be utterly obvious. This is why they knew and spoke so frequently about the power of psychedelics. The BilliBros didn't dislike them. They simply didn't know such things could exist in the world they inhabited—the world of tranactionalism, accumulation, violence, greed, domination, and hatred. They were in for the shock of their lives.

Most of the hundreds of millions watching Dr. Julia give her pep talk to *Los Cincos*, as the BilliBros nervously held small cups of the sacred brew she had prepared in their shaking hands, assumed they wouldn't drink it and would scoff at the request. However, for whatever reason—boredom, the chance to "escape," at least for a few minutes, or most likely because of the way Dr. Julia had explained things—one after the next, the right arms of these greedy men rose up, the cups touching their lips and then down the hatch, each one of them dumped the fragrant dark liquid.

At the very same moment, tens of millions of viewers, if not more, quickly sought out their own mushroom stashes at home or wherever they were watching and decided to join in this remarkable moment. Even if the incarcerated BilliBros were somewhere far, far away (or perhaps even just around the corner), it wasn't often that one got the opportunity to explore the Inner Void at the very same moment as the world's wealthiest humans. There were more than a few, perhaps even a large majority in fact, that knew they would meet the BilliBros deep within the Void, a possibility that brought immediate glee to the depths of their souls.

"Well, that's that," Puhler said, as the others slowly rose from their chairs to find a soft and comfortable place to lie down and wait. Dr. Julia had placed eye masks for each of them onto the pillows that were spread across the room, as well as light blankets, pitchers of fresh spring water, and bowls of tropical fruits for later.

Once they had all settled in on their mattresses and recliners and placed the soft-edged masks over their eyes, all went quiet. The viewers waited with bated breath. The small minority of viewers who'd had the pleasure of the psychedelic experience before eagerly anticipated the BilliBros' reaction. Would they have "bad" trips and see demons and devils? Or, far more likely, would they finally get at least a glimpse of a greed-free life, a glance at enlightenment, freed finally from the bonds of mammon? Would any of them push through far enough and deeply enough to see themselves in others, so much so that every time they saw an impoverished child they would cry for the kid and then all of humanity?

In the now quiet room, Dr. Julia—now safely out of the chamber and viewing the men through the security cameras—carefully commenced the event by starting an eight-hour music tape. The music was calibrated to change tone, timbre, and intensity to match the varying points of the inner journey—start, build-up, peak, slow down, and end. The soft sitar music matched the tunes played to those who arrived on Pacifica at the airport and these morphed slowly over time into various trance-like sounds, some long, extended, other-worldly *Morning Dew* jams by the Grateful Dead and assorted instrumental rhythms that would soothe even the most jaded of souls.

Larry felt the effects first. He first saw flashes of light. It began as white light, then it turned every color of the rainbow in an instant, flashing over and over and over. It was the most beautiful thing he had ever seen. As he concentrated on the light, seeking its source deep in the distance, he watched as it blossomed from a bud into the massive glory of a huge golden sunflower that instantly engulfed him—plunging everything into temporary darkness. Trying to find his way from within the tight squeeze of the flower, looking for a way out, Larry saw a small pinprick of light and headed toward it. The pinprick became a small hole, then grew larger, then huge—until it was a vast, open space, like an empty canvas ready for a painter's first strokes.

Just as Larry wondered what would appear next, Helmut began moaning and groaning, not in pain, but in a manner that audibly expressed the joy of releasing decades of pent-up frustration about needing to be the richest man alive. Questions burst forth deep within the unexplored recesses of his unusual brain, forcing him to ask: *Do I really need that? Do I truly need all that money, all those things? Do I really have to fly into space to live there? Do I really need a chastity belt, my Dick Chainy? What does life mean, after all? Is DNA real? Is my DNA almost identical to everyone else's DNA? Are a tree and I almost the same in chemical terms? Is every breath I breathe really full of atoms released at the time of the Big Bang? Is Earth really finite? Is climate change real? Is life actually about love, compassion and kindness? Does equality actually feel better, far better, than the world of inequality? Is being actually better than doing, actually better than having?*

His tripping experience, thus far, bore no resemblance to the world that he normally inhabited. Helmut's mind swirled with these and many other thoughts as he lay, light as a feather, on Dr. Julia's comfortable floor, feeling the happiest he had ever been.

Jasper, Harry, and William all inhabited similar spaces in time. Sometimes, it was the images. Sometimes, the thoughts. Mostly, it was the realizations. It was the gifts that they never sought—nor even had known to seek—that were found deep in the recesses of The Void, showering upon them in countless ways, that affected them the most. These gifts had no tangible form. They were not things—but ideas, inspirations. Each and every one of these men had never contemplated, let alone embraced, these universal and timeless truths.

These five souls watched in unmeasurable awe as all boundaries dissolved and everything merged into one. The selfish, hedonistic egos that once dominated their every waking moment turned into dust, strewn across the sky and into space—never to be seen again. They had witnessed the oneness of things. They saw and now knew that everything was interconnected. There was no *them.* There was no longer any object, thing, place, or person that could be defined as the *other*. There was suddenly only us, only we, only everything everywhere all at the same time in a moment that existed before their parents were born. The truth of The Void, and of life as it is, the power of evolution, gently revealed itself to *Los Cincos* in their chamber somewhere in the middle of the Pacific, and they became one with the very people they had despised their entire lives.

Perhaps most remarkably of all, as time went by into the fifth hour of the trip, the absurdity of money, wealth, and particularly greed dawned on each of them. They realized, each in his own way, that they had never been free, not even close. Money—and the endless need to have more of it—had enslaved them as much as it did the most oppressed people anywhere. Shackled by self-doubt, they had tied their identities so closely to their riches that they had lost their souls in the process of evermore for evermore.

As the journey within began to slowly wind down, experienced viewers could easily recognize the signs, reflecting on their own first journeys to the core of existence. After eight hours, each of the members of *Los Cincos* emerged back into their shared accommodation—as new men. They looked the same. Their voices sounded the same, and their gestures were the same. But it ended there. When they spoke, the words came out in a different way. There was a calmness, a sweetness, that no one had ever seen before in these men.

Within an hour they began to refer to this point of their captivity as either Before or After: before Dr. Julia's visit and their trip—or after. These five new men, overcome with the emotion of truly experiencing life, cried tears of joy as they were released from the insane chains of money. They were now free. Free at last. They hoped to one day be free from this prison, wherever it was and from whomever had decided to hold them against their will for so long. But concerns about their net worth and how much they would spend when they were finally free were the least of their concerns. In fact, if there was one thing that these five shared it was their desire to visit the Inner Void again, as soon as possible.

Helmut was the first to articulate these wishes, and after pointing his gaping mouth towards the sky, he shouted out, "Dr. Julia, please visit us again tomorrow. We love you! But we love your magical elixir even more!"

They were lucky it happened when it did. Because during their journey within, even without the good doctor's help, the world would have freed them from the bonds of mammon, nonetheless. Across the rest of the planet, and unknown as of yet to *Los Cincos*, of course, the Age of the Billionaire was coming to a quick, inevitable, and glorious end.

49

On every corner of the globe, every juncture, every coastline, on every island, hamlet, village, town and city the whole billionaire craze had mutated into something no one could have ever predicted. Once isolated and largely quiet, they were now everywhere for all to see (and find). For centuries, crafty thought masters—philosophers, sages, analysts, advisors, organizers, and so many more—had assumed the ultra-elite, the feudal masters of the universe, would always be universally despised and ridiculed. They concluded that revolution against such wealthy elements would be a perpetual threat to the privileged classes. But not anymore. In the early years of the twenty-first century, nothing could have been further from the minds of the masses than revolution.

Any shame the wealthy once felt disappeared into thin air, along with modesty, understatement, and the Calvinist sentiment of keeping wealth hidden from the prying eyes of the jealous majority. Even amongst the poorest of the poor who were so easily misled, adoration replaced modesty, ushering in the age of flaunt and excess, where greed became glory and holy hucksters were worshipped as living gods. In this new gilded age of extremes, this Age of the Robber Barons 2.0, all other measures of a good, successful life vanished. The names Ken Wilber, David Suzuki, Vandana Shiva, and those of other living sages were ignored, and replaced by those of the Kardashians, the Zuckerbergs, the Musks, and the five hated stars of the *Los Cincos* show.

The world was dying more rapidly than ever before—oceans rising and worsening storms punishing unprotected coastlines. The wealth pyramid had been redesigned yearly with an elongating lightning rod above, tapering ever smaller as the concentration of wealth went into fewer and fewer hands. For too long, people everywhere had ignored these crises, focusing on trivial matters. They had knelt and prostrated before the ones who would kill to keep their gains—the billionaire class, the BilliBros; the few thousand who held more wealth than the poorest ninety percent of humanity combined. Some saw the evil of this, but most did not—at least for a while.

As this excruciating absurdity became evermore visible, writers penned books, directors made movies, producers created streaming series, and thinkers developed proposals for a whole different way of running things. People were as mad as hell and not going to take it anymore. Yet, governments—as always—were the last to get on board, and even then, only with the greatest reluctance. No matter what those at Davos, the White House, Wall Street, the boardrooms of Whitestone, and other capitalist dens claimed, the BilliBros clearly ran the show.

This was especially true in regimes controlled by self-appointed, self-serving paranoid autocrats, often run by nasty BilliBros and serving them without limit. But despite their claims of being somehow different and superior to the growing number of despotic dictators, so-called democracies were also completely beholden to the BilliBros.

When anyone proposed even the smallest reform designed to improve economic equality, the backlash was quick and fierce. Worst of all, the resistance mostly came from those easily manipulated into supporting billionaires—not the billionaires themselves. A long-forgotten US presidential candidate once, not all that inaccurately, called them "the deplorables," although this dismissive word probably cost her the election, allowing the tangerine-faced criminal ogre to take the reins of power. These people had nothing in common with the BilliBros except their shared humanity, and their misery could be traced directly to laws and policies imposed by the BilliBros themselves. Nevertheless, they somehow saw it as smart and right to support the grotesque global rich.

But one day, on an ordinary weekday like any other, without any warning, the president of Uruguay appeared on the news after an interruption to regular programming. He had prepared to announce yet another example of this tiny nation leading in reason and real progress but simply said, "Enough is enough, my fellow citizens. Basta! This cannot go on any longer. We all know that the billionaires on this planet are destroying it, devouring it, just for more money, more stuff, and more power, and we will stand for this no longer. The age of the billionaires must end. From today, 27 August, we will be imposing a 100% tax on any amount of wealth that is more than thirty-eight million dollars. We will collect these taxes vigorously, as a matter of the highest priority. With these funds, we will build homes for every slum dweller in the country. We will build new hospitals and new schools. We will end poverty forever. We have needed a new start for some time, and today is the first day of the rest of our country's life. Today is the day that we say to the billionaires here and everywhere: 'Thank you for your cooperation.'"

With that, the TVs returned to their normal mind-numbing shows, while at least one stunned nation began imagining a better future. Montevideo wouldn't just be the first government run by a committee instead of a single head of state, as was the case during most of the 1950s, nor merely the first to legalize marijuana. No, they wouldn't stop there. They would be the first country anywhere to ban billionaires. The actual billionaires, of course, as citizens or legal residents, would be welcome to stay in perpetuity, but their assets and net worth would be reduced, never allowed to surpass the sacred thirty-eight million dollars.

Unfortunately, things did not turn out as planned, as if that was not predictable. Within seconds of the president leaving the podium, every billionaire in the country—there were just three—called their financial managers and said, as if in unison, "Get my money out of this fucking communist hellhole. I'm outta here, and so is my cash." These three, of course, somehow neglected to recall that their funds were nowhere near Uruguay, but rather stashed in a series of numbered bank accounts held in the name of mysterious companies with no known beneficial owner. Houses, land and art pieces yes, these were in the country, but cash most certainly not.

And with that came one of the largest and most prompt capital sell-offs of all time. Well over fifty billion dollars worth of physical assets were put up for sale within minutes, and every private plane was readied for departure. The president's words had commenced the flight of the local BilliBros. After enjoying a few days of rising support, the economy suffered a dramatic crisis leading him to fall suddenly in the polls. Within weeks he could sustain the public's wrath no longer and was forced to resign.

Though it hadn't gone as intended, it was clear the genie was out of the bottle. Everyone had known this would become a trend somewhere. They were very grateful to Uruguay for getting the ball rolling. One president had sacrificed his political career for the cause, taking one for the team, but the final straw had broken the camel's back. The genie of change was permanently out of the bottle—and ready for action. People everywhere were just utterly fed up with the BilliBros. History's pages turned once and for all.

After Uruguay took the plunge, others followed suit. Iceland came next—both the first island and the first European country to do the proverbial needful. Then Denmark raised the tax rate to 100% on wealth beyond thirty-eight million dollars. Timor Leste followed, then New Zealand. Not to be outdone, as it almost always was apart from football, Argentina quickly followed, as did Chile, and suddenly an entire world region, the Southern Cone, became entirely free of billionaires. The European Union then began a sanctions regime against all remaining tax havens. Banking secrecy was globally banned by an overwhelming vote at the UN General Assembly. For once, it seemed the domino theory actually came true. The façade of invincibility the billionaires had relied on for so long came to a screeching and permanent halt. It was so simple. All that was needed was the will to make it happen.

Now it was happening—and happening fast. Fifty-one of the fifty-three countries in Africa quickly implemented the 100% tax, with only Eritrea and Swaziland bucking the trend, at least for the moment. All the Pacific Island nations did it, including Tonga, of course. The Kingdom of Bhutan then did it, then the Maldives, and finally even

China. Country after country said enough was enough and the simple step of limiting wealth became mainstream overnight.

Many forces were at play to achieve this remarkable result. Fencie's books were so convincing and written so clearly that to those who read them, it seemed to be just a matter of time and that that time had come. Governments realized that billionaires and oligarchs generally were bad for democracy and that they formed threats to the rule of law and effective governance. At the same time, the world's public—largely because of watching *Los Cincos* day in and day out—was also convinced, having finally shaken themselves out of their blind embrace of the greatness of the billionaires, and seeing them for who they truly were.

Meshing each of these forces together into a single consolidated aim of eradicating a position enjoyed by only 3,000 fellow human beings was having an impact greater than anyone could have ever imagined. Pacifica, of course, didn't do it alone, but it was clear that even if the world still didn't know they were behind the caper, without Nathan Green, Jason Mooi, Amber Ness and a handful of other visionaries, things would have gotten far, far worse before they ever got better.

50

Although it was Uruguay that had started the ball rolling, "ISLANDS STRIKE BACK!" read the all-caps headline of *The New York Times* as the true impact of Pacifica and all haters of the billionaire class finally dawned not just on the many media outlets owned and controlled by the BilliBros, but throughout global society at large. After suffering for so long, the eleven thousand permanently populated islands on Earth finally gained their own power. Instead of enduring the brutality so often associated with the world's island killers, they became a source of change, benefiting not just these water-surrounded land masses but people worldwide. These humans would no longer be ignored; their voices now mattered, their shouts too powerful for even the most determined BilliBro to drown out, whether through the media companies they owned or the governments beholden to them.

The people of the islands, both indigenous and recent imports, finally started getting one up on those evil regimes, those colonizers, those military invaders, those jet-set yachties, those materialistic sun-seekers. They reclaimed positions of control—but also influence, setting inspiring examples for those who previously felt hopeless, sparking real change. People were no longer sitting back accepting their lives in slums. They joined climate change movements, demonstrating for more equality, not less. They forced tax havens to close their doors forever, making life increasingly uncomfortable for billionaires and their once ardent fans.

Thanks to the islands, the world finally understood the true evil permeating the billionaire class. It was they who were destroying the world for their own gain, literally using millions of times their fair share of fossil fuels and emitting far more CO^2 and methane than thousands of ordinary citizens—especially the islanders living sustainably. Until now, the billionaire class had controlled politics, educational institutions, mass media, and culture—all of which began to see the writing on the wall. Some truly changed and gave away most, if not all, of their money, realizing that the simplicity of island life offered so much more in so many ways than their never-ending search for more. But, of course, most did not. In fact, most of the BilliBros, fuelled by newfound fear, didn't turn to moderation or reasonable living. Instead, they went on a frenzied-greed freakout, consuming more, earning more, and plundering and pillaging the Earth further. But the net satisfaction from this short-term gratification only seemed to generate greater hatred from ordinary people who had been ignored for too long and who were not going to take it anymore.

The BilliBros and their generations of antecedents had treated islands as playthings, dismissing them as the undeveloped homes of "savages" and "Indians," as *terra nullius* despite their often-permanent populations for thousands, even tens of thousands, of years. Arriving first as part of the colonizing explorer class, they were cutely made into heroes by the countries they supposedly "created" and "discovered". They had arrived uninvited at the edges of thousands of islands, claiming one after another, often narcissistically naming them after themselves, like Bougainville, which remains part of Papua New Guinea despite ninety-eight percent of the population voting for independence, or after their patrons, such as Hispaniola, now shared by Haiti and the Dominican Republic.

The process of destruction began with the initial contact, then the conquest, then the renaming, then the inclusion of the island into the colonial pockets of whichever empire happened upon them first. Thus began a centuries-long process whereby the lives of islanders— from Bikini Atoll to Bali, from the Chagos Islands to Ireland, and from Australia to Okinawa, and so many others—were treated as if they had less value than the lives of the conquerors. They, in turn, just had to live with whatever type of rule the invaders decided to force upon them.

As the colonial age ended and newly independent sovereign nations emerged from colonial island outposts, a new hope sprang into being but was often dashed by the residual power of the "departing" colonizers. This power persisted through a co-opted elite, the dominance of mining, forestry, oil, gas, and other extractive industries that new governments struggled to control, as well as the growing influence of new investors in the booming tourism industry. Another wave of greedy corporate elite ghouls arrived on island after island, luring locals with the promise of riches beyond their wildest dreams.

Many, many of them fell for this trick, too, and as five-star luxury resorts popped up here and there, and then everywhere, with visitors routinely paying more than a thousand USD a night to stay "in paradise"—where the average *annual* income was often far less than a single day's accommodation.

Islands had been treated so badly for so long that finally, *finally*, the tentacles of awareness began to spread with the advent of the internet and globalization. They were done with being treated like trash. They were done living in abject poverty in systems they neither created nor controlled. They were done watching their forests, their jungles, their reefs, their lagoons, their everything being decimated beyond repair. They were especially done with nuclear testing and the decades of radiation poisoning that followed—of the raping and scraping of the land to reach once unreachable copper or iron ore or even bat guano-derived potassium.

"Viva Pacifica Viva!" became their rallying cry. This realization spread beyond the islanders to a growing number of people who backed them 100%. They saw Earth as a lonely island in the middle of space, slowly dying a painful death as more wealth was extracted from Nature, leaving the source of these new riches in a state of decrepit and dismal decay. This stark evidence showed how far humanity had come—and how far it could go. With Pacifica, everything seemed possible.

In their moments of doubt—when victory for Pacifica seemed elusive and the initial euphoria of an assured and long-lasting win began to fade—the islanders of the world would sit around the fire, delving as deeply as they could into why this had happened to them for so long, century after century, when all that most of them ever wanted was to be left alone. How could this be? And that's when what was always obvious to them became obvious to just about everyone, and that was the simple fact that the colonizers were jealous.

They envied island life. Everyone did.

They wished that *they* were islanders too.

But they couldn't just allow it to go on as it had for hundreds of years. No, they had to have it as their own, controlling it, taming it, undermining it, owning it. And in the process, even as they sold the dream of paradise to the new tourist class popping up around the world, they had monetized the entire package turning the previously free, self-sufficient, sustainable, subsistence-level, and ecologically clean lives led by islanders everywhere onto its head. In the process, they destroyed the very things that made the islands so wonderful in the first place.

And so, the source of envy for the polluted air-breathing, concrete urban-dwelling, car-commuting classes of the world was being destroyed by yet another wave of horror. Even the very land they lived on was slowly being undermined by the rising sea itself, year after year, due to the actions of humans—wealthy humans. *Watch out BilliBros*, the islanders of the world silently thought in unison. *We are coming for you.*

51

China, desperate for world domination after watching the Americans hegemonic empire thrive for almost a century, planned to take over not just its immediate neighborhood but the planet as a whole. The Americans may have considered themselves the "exceptional" and freedom-loving nation, but China's name as the "Middle Kingdom," meaning the "Center of the Universe," reinforced its drive for global superpower status. At this stage of its political evolution, China also sought to assert its global Superpower status. Hypersonic weapons, the Belt and Road Initiative, advanced forms of AI and quantum computing and illegally claiming massive parts of the South China Sea while creating new artificial islands large enough to land jet planes were just some of the countless initiatives underway to prove its dominance.

This was despite the fact that half of its population remained mired in perpetual poverty, living in horrendous conditions in a country known for being deeply xenophobic and lacking personal compassion toward their fellow man. The younger generation lost interest, the population declined quickly, and all the predictions that China would soon be the world's most powerful country did not appear to be panning out. This, of course, didn't at all prevent China's efforts to infiltrate Pacifica. It was only during a particularly raucous mushroom festival that Horst figured out their seedy plan. They then sent the spy packing and banned him for life from returning unless he agreed to join them during a subsequent Inner Void journey, an offer he would likely refuse.

The US continued its slow slide downwards. Since Britain's departure through Brexit, the European Union had been on the decline, with some members now electing authoritarian leaders. Things were not looking bright. The Middle East was going nowhere fast. Africa was on the ascendency but coming from such a low position economically vis-à-vis the rest, it would be decades before they could take potential control. Latin America continued its spiral downward after so many decades of dictatorship, despair, inflation, and demise taking its toll. Virtually nowhere was left.

Pacifica held a distinct advantage over all previous empires, over all previous hegemons, and over all previous dominant countries of the Global North, regardless of how they are defined. Pacifica was a place, but it was also a state of mind, a way of being. Pacifica had, in fact, become the first place to accrue power by never really seeking it in the first place. Pacifica led by example, coming into being at a time when the people needed it the most. Pacifica was that place and way of life that represented the next step on humanity's evolutionary path; essential not only for unlocking the true potential of the human race but also for saving the planet on which everyone depended.

Pacifica gave people hope. The rest of the world made people shake in their boots. That's why Pacifica would succeed—it simply *had* to succeed.

As things were progressing, this seemed increasingly true. Mini-Pacifica after Mini-Pacifica popped up like mushrooms on the forest floor in autumn, without warning, without expectation, beauty in its purest form. But unlike the fine fungal contributions of the trillions of miles of mycelia just under the surface of the soil which rose and withered within a few short days, Pacifica bloomed—and it would stay. Not just stay but grow, entrenching, becoming firmer and firmer by the day. Mini-Pacificas were not simply taking root within the borders of democracies that could tolerate such structures as long as they didn't threaten the Powers That Be too much. They were even being set up in usually isolated areas within some of the world's worst dictatorships. If they were careful, they were mostly left alone, awaiting the time when a dictator—or state they controlled—would embrace the idea of Pacifica and transform their territory into another piece of the expanding puzzle of hope spreading everywhere.

People were happier in the territories known as the Pacificas. They would lead by example, and as this reality became more and more known, there would be no stopping them. The world would not become a Chinese Empire, nor an Indian Empire, EU Empire or any other kind of empire. No, it would become Pacifica; it was just a matter of time. It would be anything but an empire either in scope or intention. Rather, Earth as Pacifican would be Earth as Democracy. Humans would be humans before any other label was applied. Their shared home was Earth, the basis for the formulation of a new global polity which had come into being as time marched on and the logic and wisdom of the Pacifican way became more and more obvious.

52

"We have to think about how this is going to end, guys. We've been pushing this discussion away for ages now, and it's time we sorted it out, once and for all," Nathan said, looking across the azure seas toward Kao. The never-ending fragrance of frangipani gently coursed through the warm air, as Amber and Jason anxiously looked on, wondering what would come next.

"Look, brother, listen to me. It's time. We fucking won, for God's sake. There are Pacificas everywhere now and more popping up every day. Everyone wants to be a Pacifican. And on top of that, there are no longer *any* billionaires on the planet! Can you imagine that? And it was *us* who made that happen. No small feat, motherfucker! Let that sink in for a second. Just savor that feeling, that knowledge. They are gone. Forever. We've got to let them go," insisted Jason, always quick to the draw, as opposed to Nathan, always tortoise-like in his replies to the world.

"You know what, Juicy J?" For some reason, he had started calling him Juicy J after a particularly poignant mental excursion into the Inner Void not long ago when both had shared the same hallucination of their bodies transforming into mango juice. "I agree, it's time. No one ever wanted to hold them longer than we needed to, and now that the world has changed beyond recognition, it's time. Boy, are they going to freak out when they finally come to grips with it! If we don't pull the release cord now, we might be accused of overplaying our hand if anyone ever finds out. This worked out beyond our wildest dreams, and in the end, it was so incredibly simple. Just revealing the grotesque ways of the BilliBros to the world at large, combined with the realization in government after government across the world that billionaires were neither indispensable nor particularly desirable, came together like magic. And just as quickly as they rose, they fell even faster. So, yep, let's get planning."

Having held *Los Cincos* for over two years, they were confident they would never be caught, though a sense of reluctance began to surface among the few who knew the real situation. At last, the good guys were finally winning. To keep it that way, they needed to act—something creative, perhaps even more ingenious and unexpected than the kidnapping over eight hundred days ago.

"We got them all within one hour on Day 1. Let's release them all together, as well," said Jason.

"OK, that's a great idea in theory, but where, how, when, what methods, what drugs, and who will do it?" Nathan replied.

"I've been thinking about this all along because I knew we could never kill them—and certainly never just let them starve. We're supposed to be enlightened humanitarians, after all. I'm thinking we dose their food with the same stuff we used at the beginning, a massive dose designed to turn out their lights for two weeks or so, bundle them on board Eijkelje's boat, and steer them to Bali. We'll dock that evil *Ream Machine* on the most deserted part of the coastline somewhere or just set anchor. Then, in the middle of the night, we'll load them onto a Zodiac, put them ashore on an empty beach, shoot 'em each up with a big dose, and within an hour they will all come to, wondering where they were, what the fuck is going on and how in the world they got there. Best of all, thanks to the new additive Shannon introduced, they will have absolutely no recollection whatsoever of the past eight hundred days. We'll call the authorities and tell them there are five sad and angry aging fuckwits on the beach or a pier so they'll be found. Then when they re-enter the world, they will find that their billionaire status, and that of every single former BilliBro, is no more."

"What a plan! I wish we could film that for the show, but I guess that's out of the question, eh?"

"Yes, but there is one final thing you can film before we end the show forever."

"Oh yeah, what's that?" Jason asked.

"We'll run the boat to a dock nearby, let everyone off, and then drive *Ream Machine* offshore for twenty minutes or so, with just you and me on board. We'll get all of our stuff onto our Zod, make sure all the explosives are securely in place, that the camera is running, and then boom! I push play and *Ream Machine* and all that it stands for will be gone forever at the bottom of the sea, never to be found again. How's that for a plan?"

"Sounds good to me, Nath. And by the way, how could anyone be so appalling as to have named their boat that?"

"Well, we won't have to worry about those types ever again, dude."

And with that, *Los Cincos* came to a permanent end, depressing billions of addicted viewers across the world. This was to be an addiction that few could shake straight away. At a sacred moment known only to the Killionaire, with no warning to anyone, the cameras turned off. The billions of screens across the world suddenly went black for the first time in more than two years but only for a split second. After a moment of darkness, the beginnings of a glorious sunrise appeared on screen after screen in all corners of the world, more and more people watching as the murmurs of the end of *Los Cincos* spread like wildfire across every society, everywhere.

Viewers had no idea what to expect. After being so used to the show playing in the background, they initially sat on the edge of their seats, eager to see what would happen next. As the sun rose slowly toward a new dawn on the screen, the subtle but very faint outlines of either numbers or letters began to appear on the screen. At first, they were unreadable, but after a few minutes, the number thirty-eight filled the screen— a number, a message, that needed no explanation. This image stayed on the screen for several days without change.

For the lucky few who kept their screens on, just in case of a mistake, precisely six days, thirteen hours, forty-seven minutes, and fifty-six seconds after the final images of *Los Cincos* had danced across offices, lounge rooms, bedrooms—even operating rooms—suddenly a burst of bright light replaced the still image. Again, with no announcement or warning, the screens of the world came back to life, and just as the collective eyes of humanity began to adjust, an image slowly appeared. After squinting and straining, billions of excited eyes saw the image of a large boat floating before them. It was unmistakably the missing yacht, *Ream Machine*. No one knew where it had been for ages, and little did anyone, other than a chosen few, know that it had been safely hidden in the natural caves of Kao, awaiting what would be its final voyage.

Within seconds, as it dawned on everyone what they were seeing, *Ream Machine* exploded in a massive fireball. The crime scene of so many carnal horrors, instantly torn into millions of pieces of debris that eventually settled onto the ocean floor, just a few kilometers from the beautiful coastline of another island aspiring to become a Pacifica.

53

Having forsaken what to them was a non-existent god many moons prior, they muttered, “Thank Gaia it ends now in 2056 and not during the early years of this century when those hospital machines were still so damn loud.” With blurred vision—just clear enough to discern who they saw—they glanced at the sad faces surrounding them in their soft-hued corner room. It may have been in Pacifica and quieter than most hospital rooms, but it was far more sober, sterile, and disquieting than the rest of the island. The Pacificans did almost everything right, but death and how it was dealt with still left much to be desired.

“Quit swearing so often,” said their beloved but anxiety-ridden middle daughter.

“I like it when they swear,” blurted out the oldest girl. “They sound so young again.” The youngest, Chai, just cried and cried, saying nothing, feeling everything. Up girl and down girl. Couldn’t or wouldn’t, but never, ever shouldn’t. They amazed even themself that they had kept the secret for as long as they had, and even more so, that no one, anywhere, had divulged it before now. With hindsight, it was so utterly obvious, but nonetheless, the still undisclosed news remained tightly under wraps.

They had promised themselves years ago to wait until the last of them was on their deathbed to spill the beans and let their children—and, by extension, the world—finally know. Having facilitated more deep political changes than any others, from the bad like Genghis Khan, Hitler, Trump or Mao to the good like Gandhi or Mandela, no one had brought about changes like they had. Remarkably, their once impossible vision had somehow come to pass.

Most leaders who changed things, for better or worse, had focused on single countries or attempts at international conquest, but not them. All of them had known the observable truth that somehow had never been collectively embraced. Whether intuitive or learned, the truth of shared humanity and the urgency of equality drove everything they had ever sought to achieve. In the end, the world had been unexpectedly ready, and it had worked.

Their focus had always been on the world, with a rather intense side-obsession about the few—nine out of ten of them male—who had truly run the show. The billionaires. The grotesquely wealthy, the obscenely privileged, the mostly callous, shallow, awful people whose bank accounts, mostly secret, shelved and nestled snugly offshore, never had fewer than nine zeros—and often one more than that, sometimes two. They despised them now, but it wasn't always like this.

There was a brief, nonetheless discernible, phase in their early life when they had admired these Earth destroyers, and, for a blink of the eye, embraced that lifestyle. They had imagined then, all those decades ago, that life was about nothing other than soulless luxury, just a shallow game of acquiring more stuff. It was a life of parties, pouty smiles, perfectly posed selfies, influencing, shiny red cars, and designer drugs.

At the time, their life seemed predestined to be one of utter abundance, of guiltless waste, of hating the poor, and of despising taxes, though they—of course—paid none. Amazing to imagine now, but they once had looked up to these people. They had admired their "success" and dreamed of living a long life like the one they all led. But how quickly that admiration had faded. How fast envy had turned to disdain. How rapidly disdain had turned to loathing, and then loathing had turned to something far worse.

"Girls?" they whispered, glancing at them for what would be the final time. "Please lean in. I have something very important to tell you," they softly requested.

The three children turned their attention to their beloved biological co-creator's weakening voice, wondering what final message they would speak as a mortal being. Knowing the end was near and hearing the ghoulish beginnings of a death rattle quickly approaching, the creator looked at each child individually, smiled with as much energy as they could muster, and expressed their love and pride.

They were sad to die but not afraid. Though it dawned upon them that this would be the final bed in which they would ever lay, they remained calm, satisfied, and ready. Their life had mattered. It had mattered immensely.

Seeing the six oh so sad eyes of their daughters was the worst part of all. They could manage their turn to meet the Grim Reaper, an event faced by all of the 110 billion people who had lived before them, but the look in the girls' eyes? That hurt. Knowing that Gaia would live on after their body no longer existed brought them comfort, as they had much to take credit for in that regard.

Just as they murmured their last goodbyes, the creator shoved a small, frayed envelope into Chai's hand. She held it close, tear after tear dropping down her face—straight onto the last thing her beloved parent would ever give her. She promised herself not to open the letter until the soothing sound of her favorite parent's words, the recollection of their smell and touch, the melody of their voice, had slowly faded from her memory like a lost memento struggling to keep the tangible elements of their memory alive.

Little did she know that this small piece of paper within the brownish envelope held all of the answers that many sleuths had sought for years. Indeed, it would explain everything.

And then, as life was leaving their body forever, they whispered to the girls, "You need to know this, my lovelies. It was me; it was us. We got away with it and changed the world forever. There are no more billionaires anymore. Imagine that. It was us. We did it. We made it happen. Our dreams came true. We set it up to make the world believe it was the work of a single person, a single horrible criminal. But it never was, it was all of us, and we changed the world forever—thank goodness."

Chai then said, "I've never heard that word before. What's a 'billionaire'?"

And then, they closed their eyes and died, a satisfied smile of contentment gracing their face during their final performance.

54

By August 27, 2072, Chai, a happy and intelligent adult woman, spontaneously decided that the time was right on what might have been just another random day. She pulled the now-crisp piece of paper from the envelope her favorite parent had placed into her hand in that corner hospital room so many years beforehand, and for the first time, opened it. Alone in her favorite little corner of Pacifica, where she retreated to climb within her own mind, she flattened the single sheet of recycled homemade paper so she could finally read it. Much to her surprise, it wasn't a letter so much as a treasure map. Within seconds, she deciphered where the treasure was buried on the hand-drawn map.

She pondered whether to share the discovery with the other Pacificans but decided against it, just in case. She set out through the hills, the still-pristine jungle—the Pacificans, being ecology-minded, knew the true value of an intact tropical rainforest. She climbed past two caves on the left, then four caves on the right, until she reached a spot she had only visited once before, early in Pacifica's history. They had once considered using this location as the quarterly ceremony control center but decided against it due to the difficulty in reaching it.

Chai was just a few paces away from the entrance of the meditation den, a cave so far into the interior of the island that only the most diligent would climb up to it. She counted out eighteen steps, found the boulder it mentioned, took two side steps away from the cliff edge, and stood on the spot of the "X" on the map. She dug vigorously until she touched the metal lid of a secure box, about thirty cm. down.

She carefully removed the container from its temporary tomb, brushed off the soil and read the writing on the top of the box:

I LOVE YOU.

I LOVE EVERYONE.

I LOVE EARTH.

I LOVE OUR STORY.

She opened the lid and discovered a thick, beautifully bound, handmade journal, simply entitled, *Pacifica: Our Story*. The first entry was dated August 27, 2029, written precisely forty-three years before:

> *We are out of options. We must do something, anything. The situation is now so bad that I find it difficult to unearth any words strong enough to accurately describe the daily horrors that confront us. It is out of control. Our planet is dying, our climate is changing beyond recognition, and yet, the richest among us, our human family, get richer and richer with each passing year—indeed, each passing day—while billions upon billions of us barely scrape by. The billionaires know all about this, but none have visited any of the world's 250,000 slums in years. None have been courageous enough to spend their money alleviating human suffering. A suffering that they largely cause.*
>
> *The problem is that we are not alone on this planet. The Earth is being torn apart, driven mostly by greed—but for far too many out of need. And so, a tiny group squeezes out more wealth for the already overflowing bank accounts of the billionaire class, without even a casual thought for the damage done to our fragile world.*
>
> *It is said that we need nature, but nature doesn't need us. However, the world I see today looks a lot different than that. Nature strains as forests disappear, ice melts, and methane escapes from thawed permafrost. Even space is polluted with disgusting, permanently circulating neon advertisements and millions of pieces of space junk, which the very motherfuckers who created them will never clean up.*
>
> *I say it again: Our world is dying. This is not hyperbole. This is not an exaggeration. This is neither melodrama nor*

hyperbole. This is the simple truth. The same place on which we all depend is slowly losing its ability to regenerate and repair the damage already done. And yes, the time for waiting has ended.

The time for patience is over.
The time for action is now.
We are everywhere.
Pacifica needs you!
Will you join us?

28 December 2029

My beloved continues to amaze me. His ability to meditate in four-hour-long sessions. His aptitude to not just take a heroic dose of the mushroom medicine but quadruple that amount, twenty grams, and still somehow make it back home with a few more insights and an awful lot of additional wisdom. His ability to stick with me despite my waning hope that the changes we are putting into motion will last. Everything about him—even his name—amazes me, but his promise today hit me harder than anything else he had ever done. For it was on this day—soon to be a holiday in our new home—that he promised to dedicate the remainder of his life to making our Pacifica dream a reality. With that promise and my cash, combined with our ridiculous gains in crypto, we have more than one hundred billion to get things moving, more than enough to create the most perfect society the world has ever seen.

With global efforts to control climate change failing, it now seems more likely than ever that temperatures will exceed 3°C above historical averages, and the effects are already all around us. And yet, the United States and China continue to churn out CO^2 *at criminal levels. Meanwhile, the remnants of gases released by the wealthy West still have a devastating impact, despite attempts by many countries to reduce them, with the dreadful exception of Australia, which maintains the worst climate record of any member of the OECD. More countries than ever before maintain nuclear weapon stocks, internal conflict is rampant, and the rise of dictators and authoritarians seems to have become a permanent reality in a world that just a few years ago appeared to be becoming more democratic. That the oceans now hold more plastic within their massive basins than fish appals me beyond description. What the fuck are we doing? Is our species even worth saving? I wonder about that all too often these days. Our insatiable materialistic desires truly seem beyond control. When I see films of tens of thousands of people waiting for the doors of a department store to open and then proceed to literally kill each other to grab some meaningless bargains, our species sickens me. The ongoing racism of so many world leaders, so many ordinary people in so many countries, and the re-emergence of white supremacy and claims that certain religions, political systems, or beliefs are "exceptional" or "chosen" appals me.*

Many of us understand the inherent oneness of things, the essential unity of all life—including human beings. We recognize that we are simple pieces of nature's puzzle. We know happiness comes most readily from things that have no cost to nature nor to one's pocketbook, and how a life of devotion to others, to giving rather than receiving, to kindness, to compassion, to a laugh and to a smile, and to so much more, we know intuitively that everything we could ever possibly need for a literal paradise on Earth is already here.

We have everything we need, and we have the numbers. We are a majority now, and we know how to live within the limits of nature and the limits of our planet as a whole. We know how to live an incredibly abundant life without burning fossil fuels, without using plastic, without buying throw-away bags or anything else, without guns or violence, without pesticides, without hatred and disdain, without nationalism or us-vs.-them attitudes.

5 July 2032

Well, we did it. I hope whichever of you reads this first will read it many years from now because none of us are ready to give up on life just yet. Of course, you might read it just a few days from now or decades (hopefully!) in the future; I cannot know that yet. We are so hopeful for the future that I suspect it will be closer to the latter timeframe than the former. My beautiful girls, you are so familiar with Pacifica—it has been your home for your entire lives, and you are simply used to it, so to you, it might seem nothing special, but it is.

I just want you to know how unlikely it was that a place like Pacifica would ever be created before it became real. It took so much sacrifice by so many to build our little Earthly paradise. It took all of us, both the founders and those who followed, as well as all of the wonderful Tongans, who continue to amaze me every day with their incredible generosity, joyfulness, and hard work. Without them, we could have never succeeded.

Please never take it for granted. Yes, there are Pacificas everywhere now, but there is only one original Pacifica that started it all. We need this miracle to keep going to make sure even more Pacificas are created in areas that have not yet done so. We have tried our best to create a society that best serves the people, the planet, and the future. We will never impose our ways on anyone, but we hope that others will take inspiration from us and keep leading us further and further into the direction of our true potential. We still believe that most people, most places, by a very large majority want to live in places where crime is non-existent, where poverty is vanquished, where psychedelics are a core part of the culture, where they are—just like us—fully self-sufficient in food, energy, and so much more.

We are so blessed to have been able to raise you all here on Pacifica, and to watch you grow as you frolicked endlessly along the paths of our island home. Watching you each gather frangipani blossoms year in, year out, and weave them into your hair, listening to your endless laughs and your expanding minds has been so wonderful. I pray to Gaia that we will have decades and decades more time, all of us.

27 August 2035

My darlings,

I wish I had written more in my journal over the years, but I at least wrote enough for you to know what you might want to know when we're no longer here to answer your endless questions. Today, I am finally going to spill the beans. You are old enough now to at least partially understand why we had to do what we did. I don't want you ever to see me, or us, as bad guys in any way. We did what we did because we had no other option.

Being used to Pacifica, even though you know about the rest of the world and how it fits together, you might think everyone lives like us. This is sadly not yet the case, and despite our efforts, it may never happen unless your generation and those that come after keep the flame alive. Though your wisdom is deep and your awareness wide, we need to always remember, as Ken Wilber used to say, that the map is not the territory. We have tried to show that the four Ps—paradise, peace, progress, and prosperity—can go hand-in-hand, and while everyone can find Pacifica on the map, only by seeing it in person can they ever really understand just how significant our territory is, and what is possible in our otherwise horrible world.

It will be difficult for my beautiful girls to ever truly understand just how deep the crises are around the world and how we had no choice other than to at least try to do something about it. Climate change was devastating the planet and the economic system that caused it—capitalism—just continued unabated. People believed that their countries were superior to all other countries, as if humans were somehow different from one another. People killed each other to have access to oil and farmland and lithium. Poverty was everywhere and growing without end. The rich could never accept they had enough, so each one fought to grow their bank balances, ensuring they had more at the year's end than at the start.

I know you three didn't have to see very much of this except in films and books and stories, but I saw it all, and I lived it. I hated it. I just couldn't believe that humanity could behave so badly, so often, in so many places. I knew I had to do something about it and try to build a better world. Thankfully, just as I was coming to this realization, I met your father, Nathan. I was just twenty-nine then—long, long ago, I know!—and within just a few seconds of meeting him, I fell in love and have been ever since. He is such an extraordinary man, and I hope all of you realize just how lucky you were to have him.

Even without my dad's help, Nathan and I would have tried our best to change the world for the better. But with my dad, it all became possible.

Girls, I am now going to tell you something I couldn't tell you when I was alive, so be prepared. Before I tell you what I am going to tell you, please accept my apologies that I couldn't share this with you earlier. I hope you will understand.

Girls, my dad—your grandfather—was very, very rich. In fact, he was one of the richest men in the world. I grew up in a mansion near Los Angeles in a place called Laguna Beach. My parents' house was located within a private guarded compound surrounded by yet another guarded compound, and it even had a name. My dad called it Winner. I had my own cottage in the compound, but that "cottage" was bigger than most people's houses, and life was as luxurious as it could possibly be. But the more I read and the more people I met, the more I hated this world of wealth and privilege. I was so unhappy. I was miserable. In fact, for a time I didn't want to live at all. And that's when Nathan came into my life. You know that story, but what you don't know is I was briefly in love with Jason, too, when he and I first became the close friends that we remain today. He, too, is such a wonderful man, but destiny put me into the arms of your dad, and the rest is history.

But, girls, you need to know two more things before I go. First, I need to tell you that your grandfather, my father, was Harold Prescott Ness, one of the five billionaires who starred in Los Cincos. He gave me one billion dollars when I was born, and that grew into thirty billion dollars by the time I turned thirty. It was with that money, and a bit extra, that we built

Pacifica. I gave all my money away, and I hope you can see that it was very much worth it. I may have despised my greedy dad in many ways, but I will always be eternally grateful that he gifted me with the tools—the money—that allowed our vision to become reality. I am sorry I couldn't tell you about your grandfather, but I hope you will understand once you think everything through.

And, finally, I need you all to know one last thing. Girls, you need to know that the whole Los Cincos thing—the kidnapping and release of the billionaires, the constant streaming and filming, and then the successful global fight against billionairism —which we won!—took place over on Kao. We did it all. We conceived of it. We funded it. We organized it. We did everything. We, together, were the Killionaire—Nathan, me, Jason, Horst, Flea, and Dr. Julia. Somehow, the secret stayed secret all these years, but I feel I had to let you know. You are innocent, and so is everyone else.

You can choose to tell the world or not; I will leave that to you. With all of us gone, no one can prosecute us now. With Pacificas established worldwide, the end of billionairism is a fact, and there is at least a chance humanity will survive the ongoing polycrises confronting the world.

Please remember that we killed no one, despite the name we came up with to make people think we were a single person with some murderous intent. Other than taking away the freedom of five people for a couple of years—all the while they lived in utter opulence—and broadcasting their plight for all the world to see, our motives were as pure as Pacifica's clean air. The billionaires were destroying the world, day-in, day-out. They dominated politics and killed people and the planet like never before. I knew so many of them personally because of my dad. Let me just tell you how awful these people were. They hated everyone else. They were never satisfied. They were mean, grotesque people.

Thankfully, by showing them as they were on Los Cincos, this proved the lynchpin in finally ending their scourge once and for all. So, yes, it was a crime we committed—I can happily admit that—but it was worth it. We had to do it, and it worked. We won. They are finished. There are none left. Hopefully, at least one of you if not all of you wouldn't even have heard the word "billionaire" before, because it is just so absurd that any single human could have ever been allowed to amass so much wealth. No one was willing to do what was needed, except for us. And again, it worked. All it took was people seeing them up close and personal, followed by a simple pen stroke placing a 100% tax on all assets and income higher than thirty-eight million dollars. After Uruguay went first, and then Iceland, everyone else followed suit, and before too long, it was bye-bye billionaires forever.

Please try to understand, girls. I hope you can embrace what we did and comprehend just how needed it was.

I love you all, but you already knew that. I am gone now in my physical form, but please keep me alive in your heart. Feel my presence when you are sad and know I will be with you forevermore.

Viva Pacifica Viva!
Amber (Momma)

55

At 3:30 a.m., the solar battery-powered Zodiac pulled up to the immaculate dock of one of Bali's many luxury resorts. Located on the far less crowded northern coast of the island, it was empty and quiet. Horst and Iene had scoured the area beforehand to ensure it would be completely empty for their arrival. Nathan and Jason gathered their things and climbed onto the wooden structure, a fresh, coconut-infused wind blowing gently through their golden locks. *Los Cincos* were still out cold, scheduled to awaken in an hour or so. They hurriedly lifted each of them onto the dock, propping them up against each other back-to-back in a circle looking outward.

In the middle of the circle, Nathan and Jason placed an incredible array of Balinese fruits and other delights, along with fifty liters of Fiji bottled water, awaiting a collective re-awakening in a world *Los Cincos* would all remember soon enough.

Their former captors stood back and looked at these five men one final time. Having observed them for years and particularly closely during their time on Kao, Nathan and Jason knew these men intimately—in fact, somewhat too intimately. It was true that these men had clearly changed following their mushroom journey, changes that the Pacificans hoped would, of course, be permanent. However, when they looked at them still passed out, sitting in a sad and rather pathetic circle, they couldn't forget the evils these men were directly responsible for. The cumulative human and planetary suffering that could be sourced to these five men was unimaginable. How just five humans could create such extreme pain and anguish in literally millions upon millions of innocent fellow citizens still shocked them and always would. Neither Nathan nor Jason could let these thoughts go. They could never forgive these horrible humans, and it was clear that the suffering they generated was not anything that could be reversed. The suffering was done. It was in the memory banks of those victimized by it.

Just then, wordlessly as always, Nathan and Jason looked deeply into each other's eyes and both knew that they were having the very same thought: Should we really spare these fuckers? No one can see us now. We could just take them out right now in a matter of seconds and still get away with it. Nathan's right hand moved slowly downward towards his beltline. There hung a sheath for his beloved Japanese blade, which measured 18cms, 30cms if the handle was included in the measurement. Jason watched with concern written all over his tanned face. While a part of him hoped Nathan would do it, despite all of his pleas to the contrary, he knew instinctively that they could not end the lives of these men, no matter how despicable they were. He simply muttered "Ah," and with that, Nathan looked at him, realized he had to be wise and then slowly let his knife go, bowing his head in the process.

Los Cincos had survived. They made it through. Governments that banned billionairisim killed no one. Pacifica killed no one. Nor did the Killionaire. But the convergence of these forces, both legal and nefarious, had changed everything else. As the five former billionaires slowly awakened, they would come to realize in the coming days, that their net worth had dropped by more than ninety-nine percent, along with the fortunes of every billionaire worldwide—all of them. There were none left. Game over. Pacifica: 1. Billionaires: 0.

In the span of just a few short years, the world accomplished what it could have done anytime during the decades that the billionaire phenomenon had kept growing. The world decided—because of Pacifica and the *Los Cincos* Show—to do something extreme and unprecedented, as more and more people came to the realization that there was nothing inevitable about the phenomenon of billionairism. It was a manmade reality, made possible solely due to the decisions of humans about the lives of other humans. Governments, company heads, thinkers, voters, businesspeople and so many others had blindly gone along with the views of the richest that no intervention should be allowed. Reducing the taxes of the wealthiest didn't contribute to inequality, it merely stifled progress, they would argue. And as capital accumulated into fewer and fewer hands, those holding it would stop at nothing to preserve and grow their wealth with no upward limit in sight.

The billionaires would collude together and select the heads of political parties. They would draft new laws and policies to reduce taxation rates, enable the secret stashing of holdings in offshore banks and do everything possible to capture the governments of the world to ensure that no one and nothing could stop them. They would work with dictators and the unelected to protect their interests at any cost. They would spend money to intentionally violate the basic rights of ordinary people. They would support wars and the production of military machines. They would grab land, extract natural resources, work with genocidal maniacs and gruesome henchmen to preserve their positions of limitless power and control. For years they did this without fear or sanction, and with each passing year the assets grew, as did the scale of their domination.

And then, almost without warning, it happened. Just like the revolutions that were impossible until they weren't, the concept of billionairism died a quick and relatively painless death. None of them went hungry. But forevermore, in line with Fencie's urgings, none would ever have more than thirty-eight million dollars to play with. All the tax loopholes were closed, as were the tax havens—permanently. A worldwide income and wealth taxation system came into place, taxing every dollar over thirty-eight million at 100%. It really was as simple as that. The grotesque ways of the billionaires were finished. Their destructive ways were over. The people of the world had decided as much. And for once, the people prevailed, and they had Pacifica to thank for that and so much more. And best of all, the planet was safe at last and humanity's survival, too, looked more and more likely.

Nathan and Jason strode toward the shore, arm in arm, a sense of deep contentment washing over them as a wave of some form of bliss they'd never before felt—something they could easily become accustomed to. For a split second, they felt they had won. They felt satisfied. They were ready to live out quiet lives far from cities and all the rest. What more could possibly be done to outmatch the events on Kao?

Nathan whispered, "My children will remember this day."

"Everyone, everywhere will remember this day, my friend," Jason replied.

The sense of finality, of "we did it," of accomplishment without anguish came over them for the very first time. But then, just as that satiated feeling started to settle in, it evaporated into thin air. Jason looked deep into Nathan's eyes, and Nathan looked into Jason's. Almost in unison, their Hive Mind formulated thoughts into words and then, in a poignant and timeless moment, their two voices merged into one: "What do you know about dictators?"

The End

www.ingramcontent.com/pod-product-compliance
Lightning Source LLC
Chambersburg PA
CBHW071615030726
47598CB00001B/284

* 9 7 8 1 6 4 4 5 6 9 2 4 5 *